ALSO BY SHERRYL WOODS

WAGES OF SIN
HIDE AND SEEK
BANK ON IT
TIES THAT BIND
BODY AND SOUL
RECKLESS

Sherryl Woods

Stolen Moments

WARNER BOOKS

A Time Warner Company

WARNER BOOKS EDITION

Copyright © 1990 by Sherryl Woods
All rights reserved.

Cover design by Rachel McClain
Cover photograph by Herman Estevez
Hand lettering by Carl Dellacroce

Warner Books, Inc.
1271 Avenue of the Americas
New York, NY 10020

Ⓦ A Time Warner Company

Printed in the United States of America

First Warner Books Printing: May, 1990
Reissued: February, 1995

10 9 8 7 6 5 4 3 2

For Heather Graham Pozzessere . . . for all the moments of her writing time I stole. Thanks for the words of encouragement on this book and all the others. And for Dennis Pozzessere . . . for inventing the perfect Civil War weapon to launch the story.

A special thanks also, to Dr. Richard Cote, curator of the White House of the Confederacy in Richmond, Virginia, and to the staff at Sotheby's in New York, for their time and their invaluable help.

CHAPTER

One

Everyone was talking about the gun.

Everyone, that is, except Amanda Roberts, who'd seen it the week before and personally thought there was something bizarre about so much fuss over a deadly weapon even if it was more than one hundred years old. While anticipation mounted among the guests, she stood in front of the buffet table trying to imagine what would possess anyone to serve tiny watercress sandwiches to this crowd. Nearly one hundred men whose dietary preference ran to prime rib regardless of the effect on their arteries surrounded her. She scowled at the silver trays of precisely arranged, crustless triangles.

"Why not just stab one and be done with it?"

The familiar Brooklyn-accented whisper tripped her

heartstrings and made her forget all about tea sandwiches and antique pistols. She turned to meet the penetrating gaze of Joe Donelli. The last time she'd looked into those brown eyes they'd been glinting with stubborn defiance. She took some hope from the amusement she saw there now.

"An ex-cop encouraging mutilation of the refreshments?" she said lightly. "Doesn't that go against some code of ethics?"

"None that I recall," he said cheerfully, leaning past her to spear an olive. "Want one?"

"No, thanks." She observed him warily. His mood had definitely improved considerably since she'd stalked angrily out of his living room a couple of hours ago. She wondered why. "I thought you weren't coming. I thought parties like this bored you. I thought you resented paying seventy-five dollars for a . . . what did you call it? A glorified picnic?"

He shrugged. "Changed my mind."

Based on her experience regarding Donelli's mind over the last several months, she knew it required direct signs from God, combined with the force of an earthquake, to shake him free of a decision once it had been made. Nearly ten years as a reporter had taught her the value of skepticism and persistence in the face of such clear, historical evidence. "Why?" she said.

Unfortunately, Donelli was just as familiar with the value of reticence. "Must I have a reason?"

"You usually do." Her gaze narrowed speculatively. "Come on, Donelli. Admit it. You were just being pig-headed. You were wrong."

Dark brown brows practically quivered with indignation. "Pigheaded?" he repeated. "Wrong?"

The silky tone of his voice would have stuck in Amanda's throat and choked her. She swallowed hard but held her ground. "Wrong!" she insisted. "If you and I are going to have a real relationship, there are going to be times when you have to do things just because I want to."

"Who are you kidding, Amanda? You don't want to be here any more than I do. All these socialites and politicians make you crazy. They offend your egalitarian mentality."

"That's beside the point. It's my job to be here. The fact that Oscar forked out the seventy-five dollars for the party gives you a rough idea of how important he thinks it is for *Inside Atlanta* to be represented."

"If all he wanted was representation, he would have come himself or suggested that the publisher come."

"Joel's out of town and Oscar hates this sort of thing even more than I do."

"Which brings us back to your presence: You're here to snoop."

"Donelli, I do not snoop. I am doing a feature on historic homes. I might not like it. I might think it's a waste of ink and trees, but I intend to do a thorough job and that includes coming to this ridiculous fund-raiser. The old

Milstead place may look like a dilapidated old cabin to you and me, but it is Miss Martha's current pet project.''

"And Mack's,'' he reminded her.

She wanted badly to ignore the reference to her ex-husband and that, of course, was the real problem they'd been avoiding all afternoon. Mack Roberts was not a person she cared to discuss or to think about. Donelli thought she should confront her feelings, air her grievances like so much fresh-washed linen. She never wanted Mack's despicable name to cross her lips again. The fact that he and Miss Martha Wellington were thick as thieves on this particular historic preservation project made her skin crawl. She'd spent most of the afternoon hiding behind dogwoods trying to avoid running into him. She'd only ventured out in the last few minutes because she knew he was probably inside right now along with almost everyone else waiting for the unveiling of that stupid gun.

"It is not my fault that Miss Martha asked Mack to help her with the project,'' she said, still determinedly evading the real issue.

"Did I say it was your fault?''

"You implied that I'm happy about it.''

"Are you?''

"No! I wouldn't trust Mack Roberts with my stainless steel flatware, much less the kind of money this project entails.''

"Your problems with Mack had nothing to do with money.''

"No, they had to do with the fact that the louse dumped me for an affair with one of his sophomore students. That does not inspire trust. Why are we arguing about this again?"

"Because I think there's a part of you that wants to see Mack again, if only to gloat over how miserable he is."

"I do not want to see Mack again," she said slowly and emphatically, poking her finger into Donelli's chest. The gesture didn't seem to impress him with her sincerity, so she kept talking. "Not today. Not ever. Why the hell do you think I've been hiding out behind the trees all afternoon? Besides, if I really wanted to check him out, I could drive over to the University of Georgia and sit in on one of his boring economics classes. I haven't done that. Nor am I even remotely tempted to do that. But I do my job, Donelli. That and that alone is why I am here. Now I repeat my earlier question: Why are *you* here?"

Silence reigned for several tense seconds while Amanda tried to hide two years of heartache behind a facade of irritation, directed of course at the wrong target. The set angle of Donelli's jaw finally relaxed. He shook his head as he brushed an utterly absurd tear from the corner of her eye, then settled his arm around her shoulders.

"I decided maybe you could use some moral support," he admitted.

Her breath caught at the gentleness in his voice and a sigh whispered through her. She took one step closer to his warmth and slid an arm around his waist. "Thanks," she said, wishing they were out of sight so she could convey her gratitude in a more meaningful way. Every now and then Donelli's sensitivity astonished her and she almost believed they really had a chance at a future.

"Have you run into him yet?"

She shook her head.

"Why not just get it over with, Amanda? You'll feel better."

"Somehow I doubt that."

"If you plan to keep hiding from him, then, how much longer do you need to stay?"

"At least until all the speeches have been made."

"All?" he repeated with feigned horror. "How many are there?"

"I know Miss Martha's planning to kick things off. Then her nephew will speak."

"The senator? I'm impressed."

"Why? You don't think a politician would miss a made-to-order opportunity like this to make points by reminding us all about the importance of saving history for all the generations to come. I've heard Donald before. He can make preservation sound as if it's on a par with ending world hunger and curing cancer. It really brings them to their feet down in Savannah. Miss Martha taught him well."

"If you already know what he's going to say, do we actually have to stay and listen?"

"Reporters don't cheat. He could change his prepared

text and declare that he's in favor of legalizing drugs or something.''

''You could always read about it in the Atlanta papers in the morning. Your deadline's still a week away. Meantime, I'm sure you and I could find much more interesting things to do.''

Only a deeply ingrained sense of duty kept her from succumbing to temptation. ''I'm sure we could, but I'm afraid we're here for the duration.''

As they stood pondering their mutual regret, Larry Carter came bounding across the sweep of manicured lawn, his Nikons and their assorted lenses dangling around his neck like oversize black jewels. To Larry, who did freelance photography for *Inside Atlanta* and other publications, those cameras were far more precious than their considerable weight in diamonds.

''Hey, Amanda,'' he called with his usual boyish enthusiasm. ''Hi, Donelli. Amanda, you'd better get inside. Miss Martha's about to start things and she wants you on hand to record her speech for posterity. She's a great old gal, but somebody ought to tell her sometime that she doesn't control the media around these parts.''

''You tell her,'' Amanda suggested. ''Even Oscar doesn't have the nerve to break that news to her and he's known her all his life. Come on, guys. Let's go.''

They were halfway across the lawn when they heard the scream. That sound, emanating from someone who rarely spoke in anything other than the soft drawl of a Southern

lady, was especially chilling. Amanda's blood ran cold.
The piercing shout also effectively silenced the throng of
people still scattered outside. Attention was riveted on the
old brick house into which Miss Martha had vanished only
moments earlier to finalize details for the great unveiling.

Amanda, who'd been dreading this particular part of the
afternoon's agenda, felt a momentary pang of excitement
at the diversion before she began worrying what a scream
like that could mean to the health of a woman well into
her eighties. Apparently the same thought had occurred to
the other guests because they seemed to move as one toward the house. Years of training as an investigative jour-
nalist encouraged Amanda to move slightly faster than
everyone except Larry, who was equally motivated, and
Donelli, who was sprinting like the well-trained cop he
once was. Trying to keep up with them left her breathless.

They arrived in the parlor just in time to see Miss Martha
sink dramatically into a Queen Anne chair while her housekeeper, Della, rapidly fanned her pale face. Nephew Donald, the state's junior senator, came rushing back from the
kitchen with a glass of water.

"Is she okay?" Amanda asked Della, compassion win-
ning out for the moment over journalistic curiosity. Joe
knelt beside Miss Martha and took her frail wrist in his
hand to check her pulse.

"She'll be just fine, as soon as she catches her breath,"
Della said, waving her apron to create a breeze as Donelli

nodded to confirm the diagnosis. "She has these spells every now and then. It's because she's excitable."

"It's because she doesn't know when to quit," Donald said pointedly, holding out the glass. Scowling at his impudence, Miss Martha waved it off. "I mean it, Aunt Martha, you are entirely too old to be taking on a project like this."

"Donald, that's enough!" Miss Martha snapped, bringing a flush to the senator's tanned cheeks. "I am still perfectly capable of throwing a party and asking my friends for a few dollars. You don't have to be twenty-two to collect checks and deposit them in the bank. Now would all of you kindly stop talking as though I'm not here."

She turned a fierce gaze on her housekeeper. "Della, go on about your business. There are hungry people out there. They didn't pay all that money to come inside and gawk at me. Tell them there will be a slight delay in the ceremony. That ought to cheer them up."

The querulous comment was meant to dispel the crowd as much as it was to get Della back to work. It succeeded. Donald stalked out of the room, still carrying the glass of water. Others began trailing after him. Even Amanda was tempted to slip back into the yard before Miss Martha sent her to her room without her supper. Miss Martha tended to have that effect on her. Despite her age and diminutive stature, Martha Wellington carried herself with regal dignity and ruled over Gwinnett County society with the iron hand of an ageless, somewhat benevolent matriarch. High-ranking politicians and wealthy grand dames of Georgia society were quelled by her imperious manner.

Although her mind was far too alert for it to be said that she lived in the past, her devotion to historic preservation was practiced with uncommon zeal and unflagging energy. It was admiration for her zeal and energy, in fact, that had drawn such an illustrious crowd to her lovely home to hear her plan to save another landmark. Once again she expected all of her wealthy friends to chip in for the cause and to make them think of it as a privilege. The party invitations had carried a stiff donation price tag, personally scaled by Miss Martha to suit the financial status of each guest. Amanda and Joe might have gotten in for seventy-five dollars, but that was definitely at the low end of the scale. Rumor had it that some of the more prominent guests had paid thousands for the opportunity to eat those skimpy sandwiches.

As Amanda turned to slip away with the others, Miss Martha reached out and clasped her hand in a grip that showed no evidence of a weakened condition. "Not you, dear," she said firmly, then waved off the rest of her subjects with a cheery—and to Amanda's trained eye entirely false—smile. Donelli and Larry attempted to linger in the shadows, but their hostess was having none of it.

"You two, out!" she ordered.

When they'd gone, she turned back to Amanda. The

bright blue of her eyes hadn't been dimmed one whit by her ordeal. If anything, they were sparkling with outrage.

"Sit," she said, gesturing toward a matching Queen Anne footstool. Amanda didn't waste her time bristling at the overbearing tone. She sat. She owed Miss Martha for helping her, indirectly, to solve a murder and thus break her first big story after coming south from New York. Unfortunately, there were occasions when she suspected the sweet old dear would be using that debt to her advantage for the rest of both of their natural lives. She had no doubt at all that Miss Martha would outlive her. She was too stubborn not to.

"Amanda, dear, we have to talk."

The opportunity to satisfy her curiosity was too tempting to ignore. "What happened in here earlier, Miss Martha? Why did you scream?"

"That was a mistake. I had no intention of creating such a fuss. It's just that it came as such a shock."

"What came as such a shock?" Amanda asked impatiently, even though she knew perfectly well that it was impossible to rush Miss Martha. She was not a stand-up comic who believed in getting to the point. She liked to build anticipation and it drove Amanda nuts.

"Patience, dear. You'll get an ulcer if you try to hurry through life like that."

Amanda swallowed back a comment. She'd come closer to developing an ulcer since living in Georgia than she ever had in New York, despite death threats and a rather dramatic car bombing. She was a type A personality living in a type B environment. Even the slow, languid drawls set her teeth on edge. She was getting better, though. She'd actually spent an entire weekend sitting on her front porch rereading *Gone with the Wind* recently and hadn't developed a nervous tic by Sunday night. Miss Martha, however, was testing her.

"I really didn't mean to create such a fuss," Miss Martha repeated, then confided in a whisper, "But the gun is missing."

Amanda knew that gun was the centerpiece of Miss Martha's vast collection of Civil War memorabilia, its value not only monetary, but also for Miss Martha, sentimental. Amanda began to sense the depth of her distress. "Are you certain it's missing?"

Miss Martha's eyes sparked with impatience. "Young lady, I am not in my dotage. Of course it's missing." Her blue-eyed gaze shifted upward and her frown vanished in a welcoming smile. "Tell her, Mack."

Mack! There were probably millions of Macks in the country, probably thousands of them right here in Georgia, but only one had the power to make the hairs on the back of Amanda's neck bristle. She turned reluctantly to meet the clear, blue eyes of her ex-husband.

"Hello, Amanda," he said. He leaned down as if to kiss her, then clearly thought better of it. "It's been a long time."

"Not nearly long enough," she said testily, scowling at the woman who'd contrived to put them in the same house, much less in the same room. "What does Mack have to do with it? Did he take it?"

Miss Martha looked disappointed that the reunion was not going well. "Now, children," she chided, "there will be plenty of time for you to settle your differences later. Right now we have a crisis on our hands. Do you realize the significance that gun has in the history of the Confederacy?"

Amanda had heard the story. She wasn't entirely convinced of its accuracy, though she knew Miss Martha believed every incredible detail. "Are you trying to tell me that you honestly believe that Jefferson Davis tucked a lady's pistol into his suitcase when he was fleeing from the Yankees? Wouldn't he have been better off with a rifle?"

"He had his own Colt and a Derringer for protection. This was a keepsake." Miss Martha drew herself up until her back was ramrod straight. "I hope you are not suggesting that the authenticity is in doubt."

"No. Of course not," Amanda said contritely. She blamed Mack's presence for the thoughtless remark. He was already patting Miss Martha's hand with the sort of gentlemanly charm that had women of all ages falling at his feet. In this instance, she supposed it was an admirable knack, but in general it had played havoc with their marriage.

"Miss Martha, isn't it possible that the gun is just misplaced? I'm sure it's been chaotic around here today getting ready for the party."

"My dear child, I did not leave the gun just lying around. It was locked away out of sight. It was right where it belonged less than one hour ago when I went to check on it."

"Was it still in this cabinet?" Amanda asked, recalling that Miss Martha had removed it from a locked drawer when she and Larry had been here the week before. She examined the elegant mahogany cupboard for signs of tampering.

"Yes, and I've had the key safely tucked away." She did not announce where, but Amanda could guess from the way she was clutching her handkerchief to her bosom.

"There's no other key?"

"None. This was obviously not the work of some amateur. Clearly, whoever's responsible knew exactly what to do. That gun was the most valuable piece I own. If they'd just been after quick cash, they'd have done much better with the silver that's out today for the party."

"Are you sure that none of that is missing?"

"Not a piece. I've had Della do a quick check."

"Then I think it's time you called the sheriff. He'll want to question your guests before any of them leave."

Miss Martha looked horrified at the possible indignity. "Absolutely not. I won't have the publicity or the inconvenience to my guests. This event will not be tainted by a scandal. I want you to get that nice young man who was

–14–

here just a minute ago. You know, the one who helped out when that poor chef died.''

Amanda wondered if Joe would feel flattered that Miss Martha had personally selected him for this assignment. She doubted it. Ever since he had retired from police work in Brooklyn, he had adamantly maintained that he was content with a simpler life. However, since meeting Amanda, he'd been involved in two homicide investigations. Maybe he'd consider it an improvement that this case involved only grand theft, but she doubted it.

She was about to decline involving Donelli until she caught the speculative look in Mack's eyes. Whether she'd inadvertently revealed something of her personal relationship with Donelli or not, she liked knowing that it made Mack uneasy. He deserved to feel uncomfortable. He deserved to be sick with jealousy, green with envy, and perhaps tortured for a few hundred years for the anguish he'd put her through. Seeing him now, looking every bit as handsome as she'd remembered, the pain was less than she'd anticipated. The desire for revenge, however, was strong.

''I'll go and get him,'' she said at once.

It took her a while to find him, but then, she wasn't looking very hard. She stopped to answer every single question about Miss Martha's health. It was the one time in her life she'd ever displayed a lick of patience. She figured it was because it made her sick to watch the way Mack was ingratiating himself with Miss Martha. The two of them were probably drinking that insipid English breakfast tea she always served with the wafer-thin slice of lemon floating on the top. Mack professed to love it.

When Amanda finally spotted Donelli, his back was propped against a tree trunk and he was holding a cup of punch in one hand and one of Larry's cameras in the other. Larry was up in the tree, either looking for a better photographic angle or chasing a squirrel. She could never be quite sure about Larry's quirky motivations.

"Donelli," she announced. "I need you."

He searched her expression, then sighed heavily. "Amanda, I have waited a very long time to hear precisely those words. Why do I have the feeling that they're not in the context I was hoping for?"

"Will you just come back into the house with me, please?"

"Why? Has someone died since I left?"

She supposed he had a right to sound snippy and suspicious, but she was in no mood to deal with it. "Isn't it enough that I want you there?"

"Since neither you nor Miss Martha wanted me there only a few minutes ago, I can only assume that something's happened. What is it?"

She lowered her voice. "Someone has stolen a valuable antique."

"What?"

"Donelli, would you just trust me and come in the house. I don't want everyone to hear this."

She walked away before she could be overcome by guilt and blurt out the fact that Mack was on the premises. Donelli was not going to be pleased at being included in this particular gathering.

Rather than dwelling on his likely reaction—or going along to see it firsthand—she lingered just outside the French doors. In a timely renewal of her sense of journalistic obligation, she dug her notebook out of her purse and went back to the yard to begin making notes about the swarm of people who'd turned out for Miss Martha's fund-raiser. She counted five state legislators, the governor, two U.S. representatives, and the mayors of Atlanta and seven neighboring communities. The CEOs of three major corporations were in attendance, along with several members of their boards. All were accompanied by their wives, dressed in garden party attire according to the edicts of *Town and Country*. Hats and white gloves abounded. Amanda felt as though she ought to have paid a little more attention to the ironing of her skirt.

The men all hovered in the vicinity of the bar, which was serving mint juleps and straight shots of bourbon at a dizzying clip. Donald was busy back-slapping and soliciting votes. Della was passing among the women with yet another tray of tiny sandwiches with the crusts neatly trimmed and the filling so thin that Amanda had trouble telling the egg salad from the tuna. At least they were an improvement over watercress. The members of Miss Martha's historical society, most of whom were of her generation, flitted among the guests like anxious butterflies, collecting pledge cards and checks and dispensing miniature Georgia flags in return.

It was hard to imagine a common thief in the midst of a group like this. Not that Amanda had such high regard for politicians and business tycoons, but generally they confined their thievery to a scope slightly beyond antique pistols, no matter what the historical significance.

She was pondering the implications of this when she heard her name bellowed loudly from inside the stately old mansion. Unless she was vastly mistaken, Donelli had just met her ex-husband. He seemed to be about as impressed with Mack as she was.

CHAPTER
Two

Donelli, standing nervously in the foyer amidst a collection of priceless antiques, did not look pleased. In fact, Amanda was all too familiar with his current sour expression. It was the one he usually wore when he discovered aphids attacking his garden.

"Why am I in here?" he inquired testily.

"Miss Martha asked for you specifically."

"Maybe so, but in the meantime she also asked for her entire preservation committee. There are a dozen little old ladies in that room, along with your ex-husband. My presence is obviously not yet required."

Amanda had to work to hide a smile at his blatant pique. "I'm sure she's just explaining the delay to them," she soothed. "Miss Martha is very careful not to offend her committee, even though everyone knows that without her, there would be no committee at all.''

''I'm impressed with her tact, but I do not like hanging around in foyers when I don't even know why the hell I'm here.'' He scowled at a graceful antique chair. ''Are you even supposed to sit on one of those things? It doesn't look very sturdy.''

''French kings probably sat on that chair. It will hold you. As for Miss Martha, she wants you to help her find the missing gun. You should feel flattered. She thought you did an absolutely lovely job of finding Chef Maurice's killer.''

''You know what the circumstances were then. I got involved as a favor to Bobby Ray. I am not licensed to do private investigations. I don't even *want* to do private investigations.''

She shrugged. ''So you've told me repeatedly. Tell her that.'' She studied his uncomfortable expression. ''Unless, of course, you're afraid of her.''

He scowled fiercely. ''I am not afraid of anyone, Amanda. It's just that saying no to someone her age makes me feel as though I'm letting down my grandmother.''

''Then say yes. It doesn't have to be official. You won't get in trouble if you're just helping out another friend. You have time. The harvest's in. You've tilled the soil until it's so fine you could run it through a flour sifter. What more are you supposed to do until it's time to plant again in the spring? Do you plan to thumb through seed catalogs all winter?''

He ignored her admittedly sarcastic simplification of his life as a farmer. ''I am not going to look for this gun, Amanda. Let the police do it. What's the story behind it, anyway? Why's it so important?''

''It's some Civil War memento. Jefferson Davis personally gave it to her great grandfather or something like that.''

''Have you seen it?''

''She showed it to me the day I was here to do the story. Larry saw it, too. I think he took pictures.''

''And? What's it like?''

''It's a gun, Donelli. You know how I feel about guns. I don't like them, no matter what their pedigree might be. I didn't even get close to the thing.''

''You're also a reporter. Aren't you supposed to pay attention to details?''

He hit on a sore point with that. She should have paid closer attention, but she'd copped out. She'd told herself that the magazine's readers would be more fascinated with Miss Martha's passionate dedication to her cause than they would be by any collection of heirlooms that was highlighted by a lethal weapon.

Miss Martha with her blue-tinted hair and flawless complexion was a product of the old Georgia social structure. She was not a woman one would expect to be sentimental about weaponry. She had been brought up in comparative luxury, educated in private schools and left with a staggering inheritance. She was a spinster by choice and she'd hinted more than once that there was a sad, romantic story behind that choice. She could have chosen to wither away and die of a broken heart or to fritter away her money and her life. Instead, she had developed a strong social conscience. She had opted to fight to see that today's young people didn't forget their ancestors. She had become the bane of developers and the heroine of preservationists.

"Amanda, what are you thinking about?"

"Miss Martha. She really is incredible. She never wavers. She has a vision and she doesn't let anyone stand in her way. She just mows them down with that sweet drawl and her iron will. From what I read in the newspaper clips when I was doing my research for the story, she's taken on half the people at this party at one time or another and yet they all still respect her."

"Not all, Amanda. Somebody stole that gun and in all likelihood, it was someone who's on the guest list. Do you have any idea if that gun could still be fired?"

"Fired?" The thought of some lunatic brandishing that pistol in the backyard hadn't even occurred to her. "Oh, my God. You don't suppose . . ."

"I don't suppose anything. I'm just suggesting that until this is cleared up, there could be some danger here."

"To Miss Martha?"

"Or to one of the other guests. A lot of powerful men

are standing around outside right now sipping bourbon. It would certainly put a damper on things if one of them were shot. We ought to get the police in here.''

''I tried to tell her that. She won't hear of it.''

Before he could argue the point, the door to the parlor opened and Mack beckoned them in. If she could have, Amanda would have ignored him and gone back to the watercress sandwiches. Donelli's hand in the middle of her back precluded that. Apparently he'd decided to take an interest in this, after all.

Inside the parlor, Miss Martha was surrounded by the sweet scent of lily of the valley and nervous, indignant clucking. A dozen pairs of eyes turned expectantly to Donelli, indicating that he'd received quite a buildup from Miss Martha.

''Young man, come right over here and sit beside me,'' Miss Martha said, patting the elegant love seat with its pale rose silk upholstery. Donelli perched awkwardly on the edge. Mack sat down opposite them in a posture that would have suited an English drawing room. Amanda expected him to pull out a pipe and light it before reading to them from the works of Shakespeare. Mack's professorial demeanor had been one of the things that had first drawn her to him. She'd assumed his intellect was matched with common sense. She'd been wrong.

''Now, Joseph,'' Miss Martha said to Donelli. ''I may call you Joseph?''

''Certainly, ma'am,'' Donelli said meekly. Amanda was

watching him regress to sitting by his grandmother's knee right before her eyes. She found she rather liked this side of him. There were occasions when Miss Martha's technique might get her out of a tight jam. Donelli was not always pleased with her reporting enthusiasm.

"Joseph, what shall we do about this unfortunate incident?"

"Call the police," he said firmly.

Miss Martha shook her head just as adamantly. "As I have already explained to Amanda, that is quite out of the question. Can you imagine what would happen if the police began interrogating all of those people out there? They would never forgive me for the embarrassment, I'm sure, and I need those people. Without their financial backing our entire community will fall prey to developers without a thought to the historical significance of some of our lesser known landmarks."

Amanda had to refrain from reminding her that a good many of those very same people were paving the way— so to speak—for the developers at the very same time that they were coughing up money for her cause. They didn't seem to suffer any great moral dilemma over their apparent hypocrisy.

"I understand," Donelli said diplomatically. "But whether it's me or the police, someone will have to talk with them."

"Couldn't you do it with more subtlety? You could just

-24-

go out there and mingle a little, ask a few questions, whatever it is that policemen do.''

Donelli sighed in the face of such naive determination. "Okay," he relented. "I'll do what I can, but I won't officially take this as a case, Miss Wellington. I don't work as a private investigator.''

"You did for Bobby Ray.''

"That was a personal favor.''

"Then I'm asking you as a personal favor to do this for me.''

"Wouldn't it be better for your guests to undergo a few moments of inconvenience than to have one of them shot?'' he said. The blunt words had the hoped for effect.

"Shot?'' Miss Martha repeated weakly. Henrietta Cosgrove gasped. Eleanor Mae Taylor turned pale and began twisting her lace-edged handkerchief into knots. Even the normally unflappable Mack seemed nonplussed. Observing the frightened reaction of the others seemed to give Miss Martha renewed strength.

"Now, ladies, don't get excited,'' she told them. She turned a troubled gaze on Donelli. "What on earth are you talking about, young man? No one here is going to be shot.''

"How can you be so sure? We are talking about a gun. Guns are often used to shoot someone.''

"That can't happen,'' Miss Martha said. "I'm certain. Mack . . . ?''

"There are no bullets," Mack said.

"In existence?" Donelli asked. "Or here in the house?"

"In the house," Mack admitted. "I suppose . . ."

Mack's uncertainty clearly rattled Miss Martha. "Oh, dear, perhaps I should reconsider," she said. "Mack, what do you think?"

Mack stared from Donelli to Amanda and back again as if measuring the relationship. From the narrowing of his gaze, Amanda guessed that he was labeling Donelli as a fascist pig. Mack had never been overly fond of policemen, in or out of retirement. "I think this man is exaggerating the danger so he can prolong his job."

A furious flush crept into Donelli's cheeks. "I don't even want this job, Roberts." He turned pointedly to Miss Martha. Amanda wondered if anyone else noticed that he was clenching his fists. "Miss Wellington, it's up to you," he said. "I still recommend bringing in the police."

"Not yet," she said after a momentary hesitation. "I would like you to take a look around first. Then we will discuss your findings and make a decision."

"I won't be able to protect your guests," Donelli warned.

"I understand," Miss Martha said. "I will take full responsibility for whatever happens."

Amanda thought the whole incident was getting out of hand with all the talk of sinister machinations and Mack and Donelli circling like testy boxers before a match. "Don't you think perhaps we're all getting worked up over nothing? I know it meant a lot to you, Miss Martha, but after all, it was just a gun."

"You wouldn't say that, if you understood history," Mack said. "For a woman who's always professed objectivity, you seem to have a real bias on this one subject."

"It's a gun, Mack. Not the original copy of the Declaration of Independence."

Miss Martha regarded her indignantly. "Amanda, dear, that gun belonged to our very own Jefferson Davis, the president of the Confederacy."

"The South lost the war." There were times when Amanda was convinced they'd all lost sight of that particular detail. Maybe you had to have been born and raised in the South to understand their blind spot. As if to confirm her suspicion, a collective sigh greeted the traitorous remark.

"It was a most tragic moment in the South's proud history," Miss Martha said, her patriotic fervor beginning to build to a feverish pitch. Amanda tuned out the rest of the lecture, which she'd heard several times before.

"Why is it that you young people today have no sense of the past?" Miss Martha lamented.

"Indeed," echoed a dozen bobbing heads.

"Except for Mack, of course," Miss Martha said, smiling fondly at him.

"What a guy," Amanda muttered under her breath as she watched the blood rise in Donelli's cheeks at the high praise of Mack. He refrained from making a rude retort.

She'd have to congratulate him later on his restraint. For that matter, she was rather proud of her own.

"It's not that Amanda is disinterested," Donelli said as if she needed to have her motivations explained for her. "I think that Amanda's profession requires her to concentrate so much on what's happening right now that she sometimes loses sight of the past. Isn't that so, Amanda?"

"More or less," she said, unwilling to elaborate on her intense dislike of all things musty and moldy and outdated. That bias extended to her marriage. Mack was observing Donelli's defense with that smug expression that always made her want to slug him. Mack felt anyone without a Ph.D. had the brainpower of an ant. He'd made a concession for her. He'd come unglued for that sophomore.

"Will you at least call an expert?" Miss Martha begged Amanda. "I'm sure once you've talked to a true appraiser, you'll see precisely how important this is."

Amanda could see that she wasn't going to get any peace from any of the people in this room unless she agreed. In fact, she had an awful feeling that if she said no, Miss Martha was perfectly capable of siccing Mack on her for another of his endless dissertations on the Civil War. She had spent countless afternoons in this very room while the two of them went on and on with anecdotes about Sherman's march to the sea, the burning of Atlanta, the looting of homes, the humiliation of defeat. One would have thought they'd experienced it personally.

"Whom would you like me to call?" she finally asked, her tone aggrieved.

"There's a gentleman at the Museum of the Confederacy. I'm sure he can explain everything you need to know," Miss Martha said.

"It's Sunday."

"He'll probably be there, but if he's not, I have his home telephone number right here as well."

She would, Amanda thought. Resigned, she held out her hand. "Give me both numbers."

Miss Martha beamed. "You can use the phone in the parlor, dear. Ladies, why don't you go on back and enjoy the party while Mack and I show Joseph around in here. No doubt he wants to see where I kept the gun."

As Amanda left the room, she could hear Miss Martha regaling Donelli with a tour of her remaining heirlooms. At the rate the tour was progressing, Donelli wouldn't get to the cabinet that had once held the gun before midnight. He might never get to talk with the guests, which would probably suit him just fine.

When Amanda reached the museum curator in Richmond, she quickly told him who she was and explained that she was calling at the behest of Miss Martha Wellington.

"A dear lady," Dr. Lexington said, warming at once. "What can I do to help?"

"I need a little background information for my story, if you have a minute."

"Certainly. Miss Wellington has been a supporter of this museum for many years. Anything we can do to assist her would be our pleasure."

"It's about a gun."

"The Varina Mae Davis gun?" The man's voice took on a breathless, awed tone.

"You've heard of it, then?"

"Of course. A few years ago, I came to Atlanta myself to appraise that gun for Miss Wellington's insurance company. It's a rare, one-of-a-kind pistol, definitely made by J.H. Dance and Company for the birth of Mr. Davis's daughter." He seemed so excited Amanda hardly had the heart to tell him the gun had vanished.

"Dr. Lexington," she began cautiously. "The gun is gone."

"Gone! Oh, dear me," he said with genuine dismay. "What on earth happened?"

"It appears it was stolen."

"Oh, my, that's terrible. Truly terrible." Amanda had rarely heard such dismay expressed by the loved ones of the recently departed. Dr. Lexington actually sounded choked up.

"I had so looked forward to the day when that gun would become a part of our collection here at the White House of the Confederacy," he said. So much for unselfish sentiment, Amanda thought as he explained. "Miss Wellington had promised it to us. I know the security measures she took were somewhat inadequate, but I can't believe someone actually stole it. She must be quite devastated. Perhaps I should call her.''

"I'm sure she would appreciate that. I've tried to convince her that it was probably taken by some everyday garden variety thief, but she seems to be convinced that only an expert would have taken it. What do you think?''

"I suppose either is possible," he said thoughtfully. "But an expert would certainly know the value and would know which collectors might be willing to buy it under such questionable circumstances.''

Amanda began to suspect she'd been underestimating the seriousness of the crime. Dr. Lexington's words were beginning to put this into a league with major art thefts. "Then it is valuable?" she asked.

"Why, of course. Didn't she tell you?''

"Tell me what?''

"When we appraised the gun for her, we found it to be in perfect condition. The serial numbers all match. The fact that it was made of steel at a time when steel was in terribly short supply makes it extremely valuable. Combined with the Dance name and the engraving to the Daughter of the Confederacy, my best guess placed the value in the millions.''

Amanda suddenly had difficulty catching her breath. "You're kidding! A million dollars?''

"Ms. Roberts, I do not kid about my profession and I did not say one million. I'd estimate the worth at more like five or six million, if one found the right collector.''

Her thoughts reeling at the implications, Amanda murmured a distracted thanks and went in search of Miss Martha and Donelli.

"Why didn't you tell me?" she said accusingly when she found them alone in the parlor.

"Tell you what, dear?" Miss Martha asked innocently.

"That that gun is worth between five and six million dollars."

"It was an heirloom," Miss Martha corrected.

"I suspect the person who stole it was more concerned about the resale value than sentiment."

"That's a very cynical attitude, Amanda," Donelli chided, but he was grinning. "Amazing how your eyes start to sparkle at the mention of large sums of money."

"Don't be crass, Donelli. It just changes things."

"How?"

"This is turning into a story."

"Oscar will be pleased to know you think so."

"Okay, Donelli. Cut the sarcasm." She turned to Miss Martha and asked something she'd never imagined wanting to know: "Where is Mack?"

Miss Martha seemed exceptionally pleased by her interest. Too pleased. A tiny little suspicion blossomed in Amanda's mind. Had Miss Martha plotted this to pique Amanda's flagging interest in the story . . . or maybe in Mack? She'd been awfully quick to throw them together.

"I believe Mack went outside to find Donald, dear," she said, adding to Amanda's suspicion. "Why don't you

run along and check. Joseph and I are getting along famously.''

"Famously," Donelli concurred, shooting a venomous
look at Amanda. "What do you want with Mack?"

"For all of my ex-husband's serious flaws, he is an
expert on Civil War antiques. He may be able to give us
the names of gun collectors in this area.''

Miss Martha looked even more gratified by the way
things were going. "How clever of you to think of that,
Amanda. Of course, Mack might very well know a few
of them personally. Anyone who stole that gun will have
to sell it to a serious collector to get anything close to its
value." She patted Donelli's hand. "See, Joseph. I told
you everything would work out just fine.''

Donelli looked as though he wanted to break things. "A
gun worth millions of dollars is missing and you think
things are fine?"

"Of course, dear. I'm sure Amanda and Mack will
figure it out and you won't have to be bothered at all, isn't
that right, Amanda?"

Amanda sensed that Donelli's temper was very close to
exploding. She didn't like that glint in his eyes one bit.
She was also increasingly convinced of Miss Martha's
motivations. She probably had engineered this theft to cook
up a reunion between her and Mack. It seemed extreme
even for an inveterate matchmaker, but until she knew for
sure, Amanda had to pursue this as if it were a legitimate
story. She really did need to talk to Mack.

"Wait here, Donelli. I'll be back in five minutes."

Despite a thorough search of the grounds, however, Amanda could find no sign at all of Mack. The crowd had dwindled down to a last few guests, including Donald and a handful of business executives. Cursing her luck, she finally retreated to the parlor where she found Miss Martha surrounded by her ladies once again. They were totaling up their take on the afternoon.

"Where's Joe?" she asked.

Miss Martha lifted a guileless gaze to meet hers. "He left, dear. He said things were obviously under control so he was sure you wouldn't mind."

Amanda muttered an oath under her breath. Donelli had been wrong again. If the empty feeling in the pit of her stomach was any indication, she found she minded quite a lot.

CHAPTER
Three

Somewhere between Miss Martha's mansion and her own house, Amanda's dismay turned into anger. She was getting tired of dealing with Donelli's obsession with her ex-husband. It wasn't so much that he was jealous. He wasn't. Donelli had a very strong sense of self-confidence. But for some reason she couldn't fathom, he seemed determined to sabotage their relationship periodically by raising the specter of what he saw as her lingering love for Mack.

To Amanda's way of straightforward, get-on-with-your-life thinking, that was so much psychological hogwash. She'd loved, she'd lost, and she'd grieved—maybe not enough, but as much as she'd cared to. Mack no longer had any role to play in her life, with the possible exception

of his ability to give her a list of Civil War gun collectors.
But she decided to postpone asking him. The emotional
turmoil of seeing him once today had been more than
enough. She'd face him again in the morning, when she
was thinking more clearly.

Dismissing him from her thoughts, however, turned out
not to be quite as easy as she'd anticipated. Walking into
the cheerful kitchen of the cozy little house they'd bought
when they'd first moved to Georgia brought back memories
that she hadn't allowed to surface for a long time. They
were good memories, too, of all the happy hours they'd
spent fixing the place up exactly the way they wanted it, of
the late night talks and early morning walks. She'd resented
being dragged away from a job and a place she loved, but
some of the quiet times they'd shared after leaving New
York had almost made up for the loss. And Mack had
been blissful with the changes they'd made in their lives.
At the time that had mattered to her quite a lot.

His betrayal had devastated her. She'd sacrificed everything important to her for him and he had chased after a
miniskirted schoolgirl. It had made her question a lot of
things about her life, her career, her values. She had
emerged from the weeks of introspection with her confidence badly shaken, but her determination to survive was
intact. The discovery now that she was capable of forgetting those horrible weeks of anger and rejection, even
briefly, was disconcerting.

Donelli's arrival an hour later, while she was still sitting at the kitchen table trying to wrestle with this unexpected mental and emotional treachery, was not especially timely. She was not grateful to him for pushing her headlong into this current bout of self-examination. She glanced up when he tapped on the screen door, but issued no invitation for him to join her. He came in anyway, just as she'd known he would. He poured himself a glass of milk and sat down across from her, pushing aside the mason jar that was filled with vibrant red and purple zinnias for a clearer view. He looked troubled. She had a feeling they were in for another one of those encounter sessions that left her shaken and furious.

"Where'd you run off to?" she inquired finally, hoping to seize control of the conversation and steer it on an impersonal course. "I thought you had an investigation to conduct."

"I had some thinking to do. It was also obvious that your Miss Martha was perfectly content to leave any investigating in your hands, once she had your curiosity satisfactorily aroused. Your hands and Mack's, that is."

"She likes him," she said cautiously, sensing the brewing of a storm.

"And you? What are you planning to do about him, Amanda?" Donelli asked.

Not again, she thought wearily, but she met his gaze evenly. "There's nothing to do. We're divorced. Finished. Kaput."

"Are you really?"

"Of course we are. Why do you have this fixation about my ex-husband? Can't you let it go?"

"It's not my fixation, Amanda."

"Well, it's certainly not mine," she retorted, grabbing a flower out of the jar and beginning to strip it of its petals. "I got Mack Roberts out of my system the day he announced he'd fallen in love with a sophomore with the IQ of a potato."

"I don't buy it. Love doesn't work that way. It doesn't turn off and on like a faucet. He might have moved on. That was his choice, his decision made after who knows how long thinking about it."

"Six weeks," she said dully, tossing aside the mutilated zinnia.

"Six weeks?" he repeated incredulously. It was something she'd never admitted to him before. The speed with which Mack had shifted companions had hurt her as deeply as the ultimate decision to go.

"That's right." She glared at him angrily. "He threw away five years of marriage for six goddamn weeks of sex. Are you beginning to get the idea of what that man is really like?"

"Don't swear."

"You're lucky that I'm not shooting holes in the goddamn ceiling."

He sighed heavily. "Which is my point exactly. Can't you see it, Amanda? You haven't gotten over him. You're still angry."

"I have had the last two years to get over him. I have wept my tears, torn up our marriage certificate, moved on. In case you've forgotten, I've moved on to you."

"Not moved on, Amanda. Rebounded. There's a difference."

"You're divorced. Did you rebound into a relationship with me?"

"No."

"What would you call it?"

"I moved on."

"So did I, dammit!" Sometimes talking to Donelli was like talking to a wall. Even now he was still shaking his head patiently.

"No, Amanda, a woman who has moved on, who has let go of the past does not clench her fists and turn green at the sight of her ex-husband."

"Just because I would still like to strangle him doesn't mean there are any feelings left."

"I hope you're listening to yourself. What would you call wanting to kill him, if not a feeling? It sounds like pretty powerful motivation to me."

"Dammit, Donelli, you know what I mean. Aren't there occasions when you've encountered your ex-wife when you'd like to strangle her for the mess she made of your marriage, for walking out because police work turned out to be more than she bargained for?"

"I don't run into my ex-wife."

She regarded him helplessly. Obviously there was no

arguing with him about this. His mind was made up and she was too tired to battle about it any longer. "Why are you doing this? Is this just an excuse to break things off with me? If you want to go, be my guest. I didn't beg Mack to stay and I sure as hell won't beg you."

He took her hand and rubbed his thumb across her knuckles, then pulled back, almost as if he were afraid to linger. "I don't want you to beg," he said quietly. "I just want you to be honest with yourself. Watching the two of you today confirmed everything I've always suspected. The atmosphere in that room practically sparked with unresolved tensions."

"Any tension in that room was between you and Mack. You were behaving like a couple of predators staking out your turf."

He ignored the accusation. "The day you can look me in the eye and say you feel absolutely nothing for your ex, I'll be waiting. Until then, I think we'd better cool it. I won't be second best, Amanda. We both deserve better."

Without waiting for a reply, he stood up, then leaned down and kissed her, slowly, gently, as if he meant to savor it for a long, long time. Amanda was trembling by the time his lips left hers. Robbed of his warmth, she wanted to cling to him, but he was already squaring his shoulders and turning away.

He walked away and never even looked back. Stunned, Amanda just stared after him, tears taking the edge off her self-righteous indignation.

"You aren't second best," she whispered, when he was already too far away to hear. "You never have been." But even after the words were spoken aloud, she wondered if there was more hope than conviction in her voice. Was it possible that he was right? Could she still be in love with Mack? Could her anger be nothing more than a cover for a deeper emotion? She thought she knew herself so well, but so did he. She couldn't dismiss his conviction out of hand the way she badly wanted to.

Donelli's ancient car had barely chugged out of the driveway when her phone rang. Amanda glared at it. Didn't the world realize she was in mourning and that at this moment she wasn't even sure for whom? She grabbed up the receiver and snapped, "Yes?"

"Amanda?"

She rolled her eyes and groaned. Not now. Later, maybe, but not now. "Good-bye, Mack," she said at once.

"Don't you dare hang up on me."

"Give me one good reason I shouldn't."

"It's childish."

That was definitely a reason, all right. She swallowed a smart-ass retort. "What do you want?"

"We need to talk."

Why the hell did everyone think she needed to talk to this man? First Miss Martha, who might not be above plotting the theft of that blasted gun just to get the two of them back together. Then Donelli and now Mack, the great betrayer himself.

"We do not need to talk," she said, slowly enunciating each word and unmindful of the fact that tomorrow she might very well be on his doorstep asking for information. Or, if Donelli was right, pleading for a second chance.

Never, she vowed. Never! "We said all we had to say to each other two years ago, Mack. Now I am going to hang up."

"Amanda!"

"Good-bye, Mack."

"Miss Martha said you were looking for me. She said you wanted information," he yelled, when she had the receiver halfway back to the cradle. Sighing, she put it back to her ear.

"Yes, I do," she conceded reluctantly.

"Tell me what you need."

"Names. I need to know people who might want to get their hands on that gun. Can you help?"

"I don't know anyone personally, but I can ask around. I know a lot of the people who handle transactions among Civil War memorabilia collectors. I'm on the mailing list for a lot of catalogs. Why don't we get together tomorrow and figure out the best place to start?"

"We don't need to get together, Mack. A phone call will do just fine."

"I'd like to see you. We never really had a chance to be alone today."

"Because I have no desire to be alone with you," she

said bluntly. "Look, I'll be honest with you. If it weren't for the information you might be able to provide, I wouldn't even talk to you."

"I guess I deserve that."

"That and a lot more, but I don't feel like getting into it. Call when you have the information or forget it. I don't much care."

"I'll call, Amanda," he said patiently. "I owe it to Miss Martha to do whatever I can."

"Your affection for Miss Martha may be the only remaining decent thing about you," she said, then slammed the phone down before he could say another word. She was too tired to listen, too tired to argue, and too tired by far to keep her defenses in place.

Unfortunately, the phone promptly rang again. No doubt it was Mack calling back to remind her of the parameters of maturity, a subject that living with a college student did not qualify him to discuss with any degree of expertise.

However, when she picked up the phone on its twenty-seventh nerve-shattering ring, it wasn't Mack at all. It was Miss Martha's friend and fellow preservationist, Eleanor Mae Taylor, her voice quivering with age and dismay. She was speaking so rapidly her words all ran together.

"Mrs. Taylor, please," Amanda pleaded, envisioning the poor, highly agitated woman suffering a stroke in that lonely old house of hers. "Try to calm down. Tell me again slowly. Are you okay?"

There was a slight pause as she apparently gathered her composure. "I'm just fine, young lady," she said tartly. "Or as fine as I can be under the circumstances."

"What circumstances?"

"I got home from Miss Martha's a few minutes ago and discovered that the thief has struck again."

"The thief?"

"I'm sure it has to be the same person who took that gun earlier today. Who else would steal my Confederate flag? Do you realize that flag has flown outside this house since my great grandparents' day? It was flying right up until the day General Sherman passed by this town. They hid it in the attic until they were sure he wasn't going to burn the whole town of Madison down the way he had Atlanta. And now some petty thief has the audacity to take it."

Amanda had this sinking sensation that family heirlooms were about to start disappearing in droves. Miss Martha's friends were not the type of ladies to be outdone. Or maybe elderly ladies just made especially good targets.

"Are you sure it's gone?" she asked, hoping that this time it might be a simple mistake.

"Young lady, I am not senile, no matter what that daughter-in-law of mine would like folks to believe. The flag was flying the day that nice young photographer from your magazine was here taking pictures. All you have to do is look at the prints. You'll see I'm telling the truth."

Now Amanda recalled the flag. Mrs. Taylor's eyes had

misted over at the sight of that flag fluttering in the breeze. "What would you like me to do about it?"

"Why, I want you to come over here and investigate, of course."

"I'm not a private eye," she said, beginning to understand how Donelli had felt a few hours earlier. Her protestation met with similar resistance.

"You are an investigative reporter, aren't you? If I called those TV reporters on 'Sixty Minutes,' they'd get here quick enough."

Amanda sighed heavily. For the first time in her life, the threat of competition did not make her blood race. "Call them," she suggested, glancing at her watch and groaning. It was nearly midnight. Her nerves were shot. The roads between here and Madison were dark and lonely. She did not want to make that trip.

"Hmmph!" huffed Mrs. Taylor, then, "Miss Martha says you're better. Besides, we don't like Yankee outsiders messing around in our business down here."

Amanda figured it wouldn't do much good at the moment to remind Mrs. Taylor that she herself was from New York. Besides, flattery that suggested she was better than a network superstar got to her every time.

"I'll be right there," she said with great reluctance. The ghosts of Robert E. Lee and Jefferson Davis could probably hear her sighing.

CHAPTER
Four

Amanda was halfway to her car, a cup of very strong coffee in hand, when she remembered she was going to need to take another look at all of the pictures Larry had shot for the upcoming *Inside Atlanta* feature. If antiques were going to start vanishing by the dozens, she wanted to get an idea of which ones might disappear first. Maybe she could get herself one step ahead of the thief. She ran back inside and called the photographer. It wasn't until she heard his groggy, testy response that she remembered how late it was.

"Amanda, it's the middle of the night," he mumbled. "Go away."

She wished a few other people had noted the time before

making their calls to her tonight. Then maybe she'd be getting some sleep now, too. In the finest misery-loves-company tradition, she said with no pity, "Sorry. I need you to do something for me."

"You usually do," he said grumpily. "What is it this time? It better not include getting out of this bed, because you're out of luck."

She heard a sleepy, female voice in the background and gasped as she recognized the drawl of her friend and co-worker Jenny Lee Macon. "Jenny Lee! Larry, is that Jenny Lee?" she demanded.

"I refuse to kiss and tell," he said nobly.

Thank heavens for small favors, Amanda thought as she considered Oscar's reaction. She would not want to be the one trying to explain to their grumpy, protective editor why his innocent young receptionist couldn't keep her eyes open in the morning. He would blame her and, the truth was, she was not without guilt. She had drawn Larry and Jenny Lee together to work with her on her last big story. Obviously the pairing had worked out better than she'd anticipated, but her own protectiveness toward Jenny Lee made her warn Larry, "We'll talk about this when I see you."

"No, we won't," he said, suddenly wide awake and as adamant as she'd ever heard him. "Now, what's the story? Did you really want something or did you call here just to wake me out of a sound sleep and hassle me about my bachelor life-style?"

Amanda decided a discreet retreat was called for, at least for the moment. "I want you to stop by the office tomorrow and bring all your contact sheets from this historical homes feature."

"Amanda, I have an assignment clear over in Savannah tomorrow. In fact, you set the thing up yourself. You wanted a picture of that woman who's responsible for a lot of the preservation work that goes on there. If you expect me to get there and still meet Oscar's deadline, I do not have time to trek into town with contact sheets. Besides, you already have prints and color transparencies of the best shots."

"I need to see everything, Larry. It could be important. Send 'em with Jenny Lee." She knew Larry's response would be indicative of the depth of his feelings for the receptionist. He didn't trust his beloved photos to just anyone. In fact, he rarely let them out of his sight. It was the one totally organized, carefully guarded segment of his generally chaotic, laid-back life.

After a long hesitation, he finally said, "I guess that would be okay."

"I'm sure she'll be touched by your faith."

"Good night, Amanda."

After she'd hung up, Amanda didn't waste any more time getting on the road. To someone who'd rarely driven during all her years in New York, the country highways seemed especially dark and dangerous. She'd once been shot at on these very roads, which had done little to instill an impression of idyllic charm. She clung to the steering wheel with a death grip, except for those few seconds when she dared to grab her now-cold coffee.

By the time she reached the quiet town of Madison, with its rows of lovely antebellum homes and lovingly tended lawns, she was grateful to see the lights on Mrs. Taylor's veranda. She ran across the deeply shadowed yard fully expecting someone to pop out of the bushes with Miss Martha's gun. Darting nervous glances over her shoulder, she punched the bell repeatedly. Lace curtains fluttered in the front window, then dropped back into place and the front door swung open.

"Oh, my dear, I'm so glad you're here," Mrs. Taylor said, hurrying her inside and securing the door. "I've been worrying myself sick over all of this."

Amanda decided that was no exaggeration. Despite her feisty attitude on the phone, Mrs. Eleanor Mae Taylor, known to her friends as Ellie Mae, was clearly shaken. Amanda observed the fluttery, nervous movements of her bejeweled hands, the pallor beneath her carefully rouged cheeks, the slow, careful walk as she led Amanda into the spacious parlor that was jammed in every nook and cranny with what appeared to be priceless antiques of no consistent vintage. Mrs. Taylor, she had decided when she'd interviewed her, was clearly a collector of whatever struck her fancy.

"Mrs. Taylor, why don't we sit down and have a cup

of tea before we talk about this," Amanda suggested gently. "If you'll tell me where the kitchen is, I'll fix it."

"My girl can do that," the elderly widow said, ringing a little silver bell energetically. From Mrs. Taylor's instinctive gesture and the bell's placement on the polished cherry end table, Amanda suspected that bell got a lot of use.

It was late, but even allowing for the hour, Mrs. Taylor's *girl* did not break any speed records in getting there. When she appeared eventually in the doorway, Amanda was astonished to discover that she was sixty-five, if she was a day, which still made her a good twenty years younger than her boss. She folded her arms across her ample girth and waited for instructions. From her demeanor, Amanda wondered idly if it required an elephant gun to get her to carry out orders.

"Tea, Deborah. At once, if you please."

The housekeeper's thin lips narrowed at the imperious tone and the brown eyes behind her frameless glasses darkened with anger before she whirled around and lumbered out of the room. Amanda made a note to have a talk with Deborah at the first opportunity. Either she didn't approve of serving tea past midnight or she and Mrs. Taylor did not get along. Was it possible that the animosity extended to stealing prized Confederate flags just for spite?

"How long has Deborah been with you?" Amanda asked.

"She'd been with my husband's family for several years when we married. To tell the truth I think the old goat was half in love with him even before his first wife died. She resented my coming along and disrupting her plans to better herself by marrying the grieving widower. She never has taken to me ordering her around. Since Henry died last year, she's gotten worse."

Startled by the open acknowledgment of such long-standing hostility, Amanda said, "Then why on earth have you kept her on?"

Mrs. Taylor appeared genuinely startled by the obvious question. "Why, where else would she go? You know a woman her age can't get a job all that easily. I certainly couldn't throw her out on the streets, now could I? She was loyal to Henry and it's a Taylor tradition to repay loyalty with kindness."

As near as Amanda could tell it was the Taylor version of turning the other cheek carried to extremes. She'd have given the old bat a healthy settlement and sent her on her way no matter whom she'd been loyal to. Come to think of it, she would probably have done it while Henry was still alive just to avoid the danger of finding her sweet potato pie spiced with arsenic.

When Deborah eventually returned with the tea—perhaps she'd had to go clear to China to get it—she set the tray down with a thump that rattled the bone china teacups. She'd brought along a chipped plate of oatmeal raisin cookies, which looked as though they'd been well shaken in the bag before they ever left the supermarket shelf. Amanda had seen larger, more appetizing crumbs left after Donelli went through her cookie jar. Obviously Deborah did not consider Amanda worthy of the best the household had to offer, which she knew from working on her article included a set of gold-trimmed china brought over on the Mayflower or shortly thereafter.

"That will be all, Deborah," Mrs. Taylor said with perfect equanimity, despite the fact that Deborah hadn't bothered to wait for the dismissal and was already halfway across the parlor with as much starch in her back as there was in her apron.

When tea had been poured and some of the color was coming back into Mrs. Taylor's cheeks, Amanda put down her own cup and drew out her notebook. "Tell me about the flag, Mrs. Taylor."

"Call me Ellie Mae, dear. It makes me feel young again getting to know people your age. Not many young folks will take the time to talk to an old lady like me."

Something about the sad remark set off an alarm. Surely the elderly widow hadn't arranged for the disappearance of the flag herself just to get a little extra attention either personally or in the upcoming magazine article. It had been Amanda's observation that society folks were not above a little friendly competition for media coverage. She'd considered Mrs. Taylor and Miss Martha to be friends of long standing, but perhaps there was a bit of rivalry after all.

"Why did you happen to call me?" she asked. "Why not the police? Was it because of Miss Martha?"

"Well, dear, as I told you on the phone, you do know how highly she speaks of you and you were very sweet when you were here to work on that story about the historic homes a few weeks back. I could tell from how thorough you were then that the story will be just wonderful. Besides all that, we all remember how hard you worked to uncover the truth during that unfortunate incident at the Watkins and Johnson Superstore."

Amanda thought describing the murder of an internationally renowned French chef during a cooking demonstration as an *unfortunate incident* was a masterpiece of genteel understatement, something at which these Southern ladies seemed particularly adept. She decided she'd better take Mrs. Taylor's explanation for the call at face value and get on with questions that might prove more fruitful.

"Let's talk about the flag then, Ellie Mae. What actually happened to it?"

"Why, if I knew that, young lady, I wouldn't need you, would I?"

Amanda rolled her eyes at the gentle rebuke. She felt like an attorney who'd slipped up in the middle of a cross-examination or maybe an eight-year-old who'd muddled something very basic in a grammar lesson. "No. I don't suppose you would." She rephrased the question. "When did you last see it?"

"Let me think now. It was just yesterday, I believe." Mrs. Taylor nodded. "Yes, that's it, I'm sure. I looked outside because Henry Junior mentioned there was talk of rain and I wanted to see if I should bring the flag in. It's very fragile, you know. I've taken very good care of it, but there's only so much you can do after a hundred years. A good wind or a hard rain would probably do it in. I don't like to take any chances."

"I'm sure," Amanda said. "Henry Junior? Who is he?"

"My stepson. You must have seen him at Miss Martha's earlier today. He's quite handsome. Looks exactly like his daddy and he was definitely what you young people today would describe as a hunk. Did I show you a picture of him, dear?"

"Yes," Amanda said hurriedly. She had actually seen an entire family album on her last visit, starting with Henry Senior's baby pictures and running up through his graduation from Emory. The album had stopped short of his marriage to the first Mrs. Taylor. Amanda was not prepared to go through that particular ordeal again. "Tell me why Henry Junior came by. Was there some special reason?"

"Oh, he just stopped in for a visit. He's done that quite a lot since his daddy died. Such a dear boy. I declare, I don't know what I would have done without him these last few months. He's handled all those technical things about his daddy's estate and he's looked after my investments. My, yes, Henry Junior has been a godsend."

Amanda made a note to track down this paragon. "And after he left yesterday you looked outside and the flag was still there?"

"Yes."

"And you didn't look again until tonight when you came home from Miss Martha's and discovered it was missing?"

"That's right. At first I thought perhaps Thomas had taken it down, but I called him right up and he said, no, ma'am, he hadn't touched that flag." She leaned closer to confide, "Thomas never did like to be bothered with it, you understand, because of what it stood for and all. I thought that was a pretty silly attitude to take, considering how long it's been since that unfortunate civil unrest. Why, Thomas can't possibly remember clear back to what it was like over a hundred years ago, though goodness knows the man's old as the hills."

"Who is Thomas?" Amanda asked.

"Well, let's see. I suppose you'd call him a handyman, though he does his share of the gardening around here too. Since his arthritis started acting up a few years back, we've hired a helper for the heavy work, but Thomas is definitely in charge. Henry said he wouldn't rob that dear old man of his pride, just because he's getting a little weak. I swear he's getting to be half-blind, too. Just the other day, he backed his car straight into the garbage cans at the side of the road, though they were sitting right where they always are on Tuesdays. Fact is, he puts them there himself. I don't know what Thomas will do if they take his driver's license away from him. As we get older, it seems that license is all the more important. It makes us feel independent.''

Amanda had to work very hard to weed out the relevant facts. ''So, you're absolutely certain that Thomas didn't remove the flag?''

''Absolutely.''

''What about his helper?''

''What about him?''

''Has he been here? Might he have taken it down to be cleaned, for instance? Or perhaps as a prank?''

''I don't believe so. Thomas certainly didn't say anything about having it cleaned and I don't think that's something his helper would have done on his own, do you? As for the other, you never know about these young people today. You could talk to him if you like. I believe he works for Miss Martha tomorrow.''

Amanda felt a stirring of excitement in the pit of her stomach. The best clue since this craziness had begun had just been dropped idly into her lap. She almost grabbed a couple of piña colada jelly beans from her purse to celebrate. ''This helper works for both of you?''

''Why, of course he does. That's how I found him, when the last young man quit without giving a bit of notice. Can you imagine? Doesn't anyone teach young people today about responsibility?''

''Sometimes the lessons just don't take,'' Amanda admitted, though she badly wanted to defend young people.

They seemed to be getting a very bad reputation in Mrs. Taylor's eyes. She decided she'd better stick to the point or they'd be rambling all night. "What's his name?"

"Clement, I believe. Yes, that's it. Clement Washington. A very polite boy. Always prompt. Thomas has had no complaints about his work either."

"Still, I think I'll have a talk with him tomorrow at Miss Martha's. He might remember something."

"You will be careful what you say, won't you? I don't want you to go upsetting him. Good help like that is getting harder and harder to find."

Amanda wondered if this particular helper was working his way from house to house robbing these dear little old ladies blind. Still, it did seem odd that a yard worker would know the potential value of a Civil War gun and a Confederate flag. Wouldn't he be more inclined to abscond with the family silver? A VCR? Maybe a handful of jewels?

"Mrs. Taylor . . ."

"Ellie Mae, dear."

"Right, Ellie Mae. Have you checked to see if anything else is missing?"

"I haven't gone through the house from top to bottom, if that's what you mean."

"Do you keep jewelry in the house?"

"A few favorite pieces, but they're locked away in the safe. The rest is in a safety deposit box down at the bank. I don't know what good it does keeping it way across town, but Henry Junior insisted. If you ask me that wife of his probably sneaks in there, takes it out and wears it from time to time. Not that I'd mind, if she asked, you understand.''

"Of course not," Amanda murmured. "Have you checked to make certain the pieces you kept here are still locked up?''

Mrs. Taylor's fingers fluttered to her lips. "Oh, my," she whispered, her expression horrified. She wrapped one hand around the diamond and emerald rings that graced her left hand, as if to protect them from thievery.

"Please, don't get upset," Amanda said more gently. "It's just a precaution. But why don't you check, Ellie Mae. I'll wait here."

While Ellie Mae was out of the room, Amanda decided to risk her neck by ringing the little silver bell. When Deborah appeared in the doorway, she said, "Deborah, I wonder if I might ask you a couple of questions." She rushed on before the sullen housekeeper could turn her down. "Did you happen to notice when Mrs. Taylor's flag was last in the yard?''

The woman's lips pursed disapprovingly. "It's a wonder that old thing hasn't been stripped down long ago. I tried telling Mr. Taylor years ago when that woman first moved in that that flag is just an inflammatory reminder of the past. There's no need for it. None at all, that I can see, but he wouldn't listen.''

"But do you remember when it was last there?''

"No. I try my very best not to pay it no mind."

"And what do you think of Clement? Has he done any work for you or does he just work for Thomas?"

"The boy comes into the kitchen for his lunches. He's all right, I expect. Hasn't given me no trouble. Leastways, he's polite enough. Somebody taught the boy some manners."

"You haven't noticed anything missing after he's been inside the house, have you?"

Deborah's face flushed with indignation. "That boy's not gonna be taking anything from my kitchen, leastways while I'm around to stop it."

"But have you ever left him alone in there?"

"Not for a second. You don't walk off and leave a rooster flapping around in the henhouse, unless you want to advertise for trouble. Leastways, that's how I see it."

"Well, thank you very much, Deborah. You've been very helpful."

Deborah stood planted right where she was and fiddled with her apron. "If you don't mind me saying so, miss, I think you're making a big hullaballoo over nothing here. Miz Taylor is getting along in years now and her memory's not quite what it used to be. Leastways, it seems to me you're not taking that into account. Could be you're getting all het up over nothing."

In Amanda's opinion, Mrs. Taylor's mind was sharp as a tack, despite the way her conversations wandered. She wondered why Deborah wanted her to think otherwise.

"Are you saying you think that flag isn't missing after all?"

"Could be it's just misplaced. I'm not saying it is, mind you, just that it could be."

"Thank you, Deborah," Amanda said and sat back to ponder that possibility as she waited for Ellie Mae to return.

When she came back, her relief was evident. "There's not a thing missing from the safe," she assured Amanda. "I've checked it all against my list. I keep it separately. It's something the insurance company suggested."

"Are all of your jewels and antiques listed in a rider on your insurance policy?"

"Yes, indeed. The company insisted. Of course, some things are priceless. I don't care what dollar value they tack on it. No matter what, I'll never be able to replace that flag. Even if I could find another one just like it, it wouldn't be the same as knowing that this one once flew at my great granddaddy's place and that Jefferson Davis himself once rode by and saw it."

Her eyes grew misty with sentiment and Amanda decided to beat a hasty retreat before she found herself with a distraught and inconsolable octogenarian on her hands. "I'll do the best I can with this, Mrs. Taylor, and I'll be in touch the minute I learn anything more."

"You won't be writing about this in your article, will you?"

Amanda hated to sacrifice a story before she even knew

the details, so she responded with caution. "Let's just see what we find before we worry about that."

"Whatever you think is best, dear."

As exhausted and drained as she was, Amanda had no idea what was best. She considered herself lucky to get home in one piece. After an extraordinarily brief amount of sleep, she dragged herself into Atlanta to take a look at Larry's pictures.

When she emerged from the elevator, Jenny Lee tried to disappear behind the reception desk.

"You can't hide from me," Amanda said, leaning over to watch Jenny Lee hunt for the pen she'd dropped, probably intentionally. "We need to talk about Larry."

Jenny Lee sat right up and managed her perkiest, most guileless smile. "Oh, hi, Amanda. I've got those pictures for you."

As a diversionary tactic, it was darned good. Jenny Lee knew there was very little that could keep Amanda from pouncing on clues to the exclusion of the rest of the world. She took the proffered manila envelope, weighed her next move, and finally shrugged. "I guess you're old enough to know what you're doing."

Jenny Lee looked relieved. "He really is a great guy, Amanda."

"That is not what you thought when you met him."

"Oh, I was just mad because he kept treating me like such a kid."

"Which you are."

She drew herself up to her full five feet two inches. "I am twenty-three. Well, almost twenty-three."

"Definitely ancient," Amanda agreed wryly. "Look, I know Larry is a great guy. He's one of my best friends, but he's also a dedicated bachelor. I just don't want you to get hurt."

"He would never hurt me, Amanda. He's just the sweetest man. Do you know that last night he even let me wear his Atlanta Braves T-shirt, his very favorite one."

"That's love, all right."

"Come on, Amanda. Don't be such an old grump. You know how important that shirt is to him. He wouldn't let me wear it if he didn't really care."

Amanda supposed marriages had been built on less. Her personal track record indicated that this was one area in which she probably should not be giving advice. "Just take your time, Jenny Lee. You know how you rush headlong into things."

"But that's the best way to experience life, Amanda. How're you ever gonna do anything really exciting unless you take a few chances? You take chances all the time."

"Right," she agreed ruefully. "And just look where it's gotten me." She left before Jenny Lee could see the tears that were welling up.

At her desk, she ate every tangerine jelly bean she could find in the jar. As a binge, it was only moderate consolation. As breakfast, it was definitely nutritionally deficient. When she was satisfied that she was not going to get all teary-eyed and hysterical, she took out her magnifying loupe and studied the contact sheets hoping that something would click, some little detail that would tie everything together. Besides the gun and the flag, there were only a handful of other items from the Civil War. Was that the link? Was there a crazed Yankee on the loose, trying to win one last battle against these Southern ladies?

At that crazy thought, she knew it was definitely time to get some sleep. Maybe after a good long nap, she'd be able to make sense of the two thefts.

As she began the long drive back home, her thoughts turned automatically to Donelli. She wished she could talk to him about what was happening. He had a way of getting her on track, even when all he meant to do was to keep her from jumping straight into danger. Evading his tactics of restraint seemed to keep her more focused. After the fight they'd had about Mack, though, she absolutely refused to go running to him now. If he wanted to spend a few days sulking like a jealous lover just because she'd spoken to her ex-husband, so be it. It wasn't as though she'd wanted to talk to Mack about anything personal. It sure as hell wasn't as though she'd wanted him back in her life. She didn't care if she never saw the two-timing louse again. She did, however, care all too much about whether she saw Donelli. She just couldn't see him on his terms, at the moment.

That didn't mean she couldn't take a slight detour past

his farm, though. Maybe the atmosphere alone would do the trick. Maybe he'd be outside ploughing up dust or whatever a farmer did this time of the year and she could catch a glimpse of him. He had picked the last of his harvest weeks ago. Donelli's little roadside vegetable and fruit stand had been shuttered for the winter. She pulled to a stop across the road and stared at it. Just looking at the fresh produce sign with its cheerful colors and slightly crooked lettering made her feel nostalgic, even though the sight of it and what it suggested about Donelli's lack of ambition normally made her blood boil.

"Donelli, you jerk, why'd you have to go and walk out on me?" she murmured to nobody in particular.

"Talking to yourself, Amanda?" Donelli asked, appearing out of nowhere.

The uncommonly gentle tone was almost her undoing. She swiped at a traitorous tear and glared at him. "Where'd you come from?"

"I live here. What about you?"

"I was just passing by and I . . . I got something in my eye. I had to stop for a minute."

"Convenient."

"Go to hell."

He leaned down and peered more closely at her. "Are you okay? Do you want to talk about this some more?"

"Not unless you're over this crazy fixation you have about Mack and me."

"Are you over it?" he inquired pointedly.

Amanda sighed. Resignation sapped the fight right out of her. "I guess nothing's changed."

"Apparently not," he said, but she thought she detected the slightest hint of regret in his voice.

"I don't suppose you'd like to get in for a minute and talk about this story I'm working on?"

"I don't think so, Amanda."

"Another Civil War antique is missing." She was not above a little professional titillation. "Someone stole Mrs. Taylor's Confederate flag."

"I'm sorry to hear that."

"That's all you have to say?"

"Not quite."

She looked at him hopefully.

"Be careful, Amanda."

Then he settled his beat-up old straw hat on the back of his head and walked off across the field. In sheer frustration, Amanda leaned on the horn. The noise shattered the oppressive stillness, the shrill sound as inappropriate and jarring as a car alarm outside a church. Even so, doing something to express her anger made her feel better. It gave her the illusion of being in control when she knew perfectly well that she wasn't.

Just to prove it, Donelli didn't even turn around.

CHAPTER

Five

Dealing with sweet little old ladies, overbearing house-keepers, and missing antiques was exhausting at best. Having Donelli walk out on her twice in one day was not only difficult on her ego, but also infuriating. Neither compared to coming home a few days later to find her ex-husband slouched down in an easy chair in her living room. It was absolutely the last straw. Amanda was beginning to understand how normally peaceful people suddenly went on murderous rampages.

"How'd you get in?" she asked, still standing warily in the doorway. She wasn't at all sure she cared to be in the same room with him, at least not in her present mood. Hell, she corrected, not ever.

"I still have my key."

"Turn it over."

"You don't seem happy to see me, Amanda." Obviously, he'd been around Miss Martha and the others just enough to adopt their penchant for understatement.

"I wouldn't be happy to see you if you held the only ticket on a sure trip to heaven."

He smiled. "Actually, that's pretty close to why I'm here."

"Not unless you've changed a lot. Now get out." She pointed in the direction she had in mind in case he'd forgotten the way.

His smile faded. "Don't you even want to hear why I've come?"

"Not especially."

"Your reporting skills must be slipping, then."

"Are you saying this is not a social call, that you have come here for something besides harassment?"

"I never harassed you, Amanda," he said wearily, removing his horn-rimmed glasses and tucking them in his jacket pocket. Considering how nearsighted he was without them, she guessed he didn't want to watch her turn purple with rage.

"No," she agreed, working her way toward purple. "You just dragged me a thousand miles from a city and job I loved, stuck me out in the boondocks, then left me for some kid who probably couldn't find her way across campus without help. How is Debra Lynn, by the way, or was it Barbie? Doesn't she mind your being out at night visiting your ex-wife?"

"Sarcasm doesn't become you, Amanda. It was Kate and I haven't the faintest idea how she is. I haven't seen her in months."

"Which one of you came to your senses first?"

"Does it matter?"

"Not really. Okay, you're not here to gloat about your romance or to chat about old times. Tell me why you are here and then go away."

"Amanda, come in and sit down. You look as though you're dead on your feet."

"How sweet of you to notice. Just talk, Mack, or leave. I don't care which you do, but hurry up. I've had a hell of a week and I'm losing my patience."

He threw up his hands in a familiar gesture of resignation. "Okay, have it your way, Amanda. You always did."

"What the hell is that supposed to mean?" she said furiously, then decided she was not going to allow the man to get off the track again. "Never mind. Let's just stick to the point."

"Which is?"

"What you're doing here."

"I found Miss Martha's gun."

If he'd declared the discovery of a cure for cancer, she wouldn't have been any more astonished. Mack was not known for his powers of observation in the real world. He preferred the rarified atmosphere of academe or the dusty pages of old books to gritty reality. He was especially fond of long columns of figures. Pondering the national debt and its alternative solutions left him positively rapturous. However, before a bomb blast had ripped apart her car in New York, she hadn't even been sure he was remotely aware of the dangers in what she did for a living.

"You found it?" she said with what she considered to be understandable incredulity. "Where?"

"I thought that might get your attention," he said with equal parts sarcasm and amusement. "It's nice to see that your priorities haven't shifted in all this time. You still can't resist a hot news flash above all else."

"Mack, just spill the details before I lose what's left of my patience."

"I talked to a few collectors. Word's beginning to spread that a gun is about to go on sale through Willoughby's."

Amanda recognized the name. It was a New York auction house that was as staid and reputable as Sotheby's or Christie's. "Have you called them?"

"Yes. I didn't say anything about the theft. I just asked if it was true that they were expecting to include a gun like this in an upcoming sale. They said it should be in the next catalog, which I'll be receiving in a few weeks."

"Have you told Miss Martha?"

"No, I wanted to tell you first."

She stared at him. "Why? Miss Martha's your friend.

You know what a relief this will be for her. She can go straight up to New York and identify it and get it back before this goes any further.''

Mack looked slightly guilty. "I guess I wasn't really thinking about Miss Martha, when I heard. All I could think about was getting the information to you. I've been waiting around here for hours.''

"Why?"

"Call it a peace offering.''

"Why?'' She knew she had a broader range of questioning skills, but this one seemed to be the only query that mattered.

"I guess I was hoping maybe we could be friends again.''

There was the slightest hesitation in his voice. Amanda actually thought she detected both hope and vulnerability in the depths of his eyes. It threw her just enough to make her ask why again, when what she should have been doing was ushering him straight out the door now that she had this latest piece of evidence. Resisting Mack when he was intent on being charming had never been one of her best attributes. It was what had gotten them married in the first place, despite enough significant differences in personality to set up warning flags that even a love-blinded fool should have been able to read.

He leaned forward and propped his elbows on his knees. She recognized the posture. Whenever Mack had been talking intensely, whenever he'd wanted to convey sincerity, he'd sat just that way. Seeing him do it now made her nervous. She had a feeling she wasn't ready for what was likely to come next.

"Amanda, I know you're tired and this isn't the best time to talk, but I really want you to know that what happened between us was a big mistake. I knew that the minute I'd moved out. Hell, I probably knew from the minute I got involved with Kate, but once things started happening, there didn't seem to be any way to stop them."

The apology sounded sincere, but the words kept reminding her of the painful reality of his actions. "Did you consider saying no, Mack? I hear it's a one-syllable word that's often used to stop things from going too far. Or were you the one doing the asking back then? You were the one who started the affair, weren't you? After all, you were a thirty-two-year-old professor and she was a nineteen-year-old sophomore. Surely you were the one with the brains, the power, the options."

He looked chagrined. It was one of his more appealing expressions. "You would have thought that, wouldn't you? Amanda, I'm not the first man ever to go through a mid-life crisis and make stupid decisions."

She clung tenaciously to a last shred of sanity. She did not want to buy into this sudden display of remorse. "Am I supposed to forgive you for being a typical male jerk? That's too easy, Mack. That's a kid's argument: Everyone else is doing it, why can't I? Adults are supposed to know better."

He winced at the insult. "Things are always so clear for you. Black or white. Right or wrong. Maybe it makes you a better reporter, but it's hell on personal relationships."

Now it was Amanda's turn to wince. Maybe she had been rigid at times. She couldn't seem to recall specific instances. Right now, though, Mack was obviously using her flaws as a way to justify his own actions. She was about to tell him just that, when he then took a deep breath and blurted, "I still love you, Amanda. That's why I came here myself to tell you what I'd found. I want us to have another chance."

Amanda started shaking her head midway through his declaration and she didn't let up after he'd stopped. "No way, Mack," she said adamantly, not caring that she was being every bit as unyielding as he'd declared her to be. "You had your chance. You blew it."

"Is it because you're involved with someone else? That ex-cop?"

Either the man had a monumental ego or difficulty hearing. "I am not involved with Donelli or anyone else. This is just between you and me. I'm turning you down because I don't trust you."

To her amazement, that drew a faint smile. Her voice had obviously lacked conviction. Her gaze narrowed, she waited for his rebuttal.

"Interesting," he observed.

"What does that mean?"

"You didn't say you weren't in love with me. You said you didn't trust me."

Oh, hell, she thought angrily. "It's the same thing in my book," she said, trying to rally.

"Nope. I don't see it that way."

"And you're such an expert?"

"On you? Yes, I think I am. You're angry with me. You still feel betrayed and you have every right to, but you don't give your love easily. Once you do, though, you don't take it back." His expression softened. A teasing glimmer lit blue eyes that had once enchanted her. They still lured, but now she knew better.

"Remember Felix?" he said.

She groaned unwillingly. "I'd rather not."

"You hated that cat from the minute it followed you home. You swore we were not going to take it in. You pitched a fit about the very idea of putting milk on the stoop for it. You said it would only encourage the cat to hang around."

"I was right," she grumbled defensively, but she knew all too well how the story ended.

"Oh, you were right, all right. After you started slipping the cat gourmet kitty food, he wouldn't have been budged by an earthquake. The next thing I knew, that damn cat was sleeping in our bed."

"It was cold out," she reminded him.

"In our bed, Amanda. It was perfectly warm in the

living room or the kitchen, but that damn cat liked my pillow.''

Despite herself, she giggled at the memory of the nightly battles between Mack and Felix over that pillow. She'd finally had to buy Mack another one. "Okay, so Felix got to me. What does that prove?"

"If that raggedy ruffian of a cat could win you over, then I can, too."

"Oh, Mack," she said with a sigh. "It's not the same. Please, don't even try."

"Why?" he said gently. "Because you're afraid I might succeed?"

She wanted to say no. She wanted to scream at the top of her lungs that there was no way in hell he could ever make her forget what he'd done to her, but she couldn't get the one simple word out. Maybe saying no wasn't so damned easy, after all. She thought of what Donelli had said earlier. Maybe she owed it to him and to herself most of all to find out if Mack was right, if she was still in love with him.

"I'm not saying I buy what you're saying," she said finally. "But maybe we can call a truce." The prospect of letting go of the hatred and anger she'd bottled up inside was surprisingly freeing. A knot that had been twisted inside for two years finally began to unravel.

"It's a start." He sat back. To his credit, he did not look victorious. If he had, she might have had the gumption to throw him out on his ear, but instead he merely looked relieved.

"What are you going to do about Miss Martha's gun?" he said, wisely changing the subject to something safely neutral.

"I'll call the auction house in the morning and find out how they got it. I wonder if Mrs. Taylor's flag will turn up there."

"What does Mrs. Taylor's flag have to do with anything?"

Amanda explained.

"You think there's a connection?"

"Obviously. The thefts took place within a few hours of each other. Both items taken were Civil War antiques. Don't you think it has to be more than coincidence?"

"I suppose. Do you have any leads?"

"They both share the same gardener's helper. I haven't talked to him yet, but I can't imagine that some kid is savvy enough to know that that gun is worth a fortune and then to get it to an auction house in New York. I'm going over to see him tomorrow anyway. It's always possible that somebody is setting him up and paying him to do the robberies."

Mack nodded. "Do you need any help?"

Surprised, she shook her head. "No, but thanks for asking and thanks for tracking down the gun."

"Have dinner with me tomorrow?"

"I don't think so, Mack."

"Soon, though?"

"We'll see."

He took his glasses out of his jacket and slid them back on as he stood up. He shoved his hands in his pockets. "I'll call you."

She nodded.

"Soon," he said.

"Whatever."

"Good night, Amanda."

"Good night, Mack."

Even though there seemed to be nothing left to say, Mack lingered, watching her. Chaotic thoughts went through her mind as she waited for him to go. Images of Donelli were all tangled up with memories of Mack and her marriage. Nostalgia, she told herself pointedly, always wore rose-colored glasses. Her marriage, even before Mack had walked out, had hardly been storybook caliber.

"Remember that," she muttered.

Mack chuckled. "I see you still have some of your best conversations with yourself," he said. He shook his head and his expression suddenly turned sober. "That always used to drive me crazy. I figured if I was in the room you could talk things over with me. Instead, you always shut me out."

Stunned by the genuine hurt in his voice, she said, "It was never that I didn't want to talk to you, Mack. Talking to myself is just the way I work things through. Half the time I don't even realize I've said something out loud."

"Like now."

She shrugged. "Like now."

"I guess I shouldn't knock it. You did some damn fine reporting with the help of your alter ego."

"Thank you."

"It's the truth. I was always very proud of you."

"You were?"

"Of course I was. Not because you were a media celebrity, but because you worked hard and you really cared about things that were important. The risks made me a little crazy, but I always figured trying to get you not to take chances would have been like asking you to cut off your arm. I knew how much I was making you give up by bringing you down here, but I didn't want to admit it. I figured you were too good to be without a job for long. When you got that first job with Oscar at the *Gazette*, I figured everything would be fine."

"I was working for a dinky country weekly writing quilting circle roundups. Did you honestly expect me to be happy?"

"I tried not to think about it. Besides, it didn't last all that long. Look where you are now. You're in on the ground floor of an exciting new magazine. You're back to doing exactly the kind of stories you love, digging for answers."

"I'm not sure writing about antebellum homes qualifies as investigative journalism."

"It does now that things are vanishing," Mack reminded her.

She stared at him suspiciously. "I don't suppose you and Miss Martha conspired to arrange that, just to bring you and me back together."

He stared at her in astonishment. "I would never play games with your career that way. Why would you think that?" •

"Maybe the way all of this is conveniently happening just now when you're at loose ends emotionally."

"I am not at loose ends. I've just finally come to my senses. As for my meddling in this investigation, I'm only doing it at your request, remember? I would do anything, if I thought it would help you out, personally or for a story."

That much of the memory was true: Mack always had been extraordinarily supportive, even when danger had threatened to explode their secure little world. Donelli was more of a worrier, more inclined to want to protect her at all costs. Which attitude was more indicative of love? It was far too late and her emotions were in too much turmoil to decide that tonight.

She met Mack's steady gaze, but before she could open her mouth to tell him to go he dragged a hand from his pocket and gave her a jaunty wave. "I'm out of here. I'll talk to you tomorrow."

As she watched him go, relief mingled with gut-churning

confusion. She could practically hear Donelli whispering in her ear, "I told you so."

Clement Washington was a cocky bastard. Amanda took an almost instant dislike to the swaggering kid, who looked to be about twenty. She found him in Miss Martha's rose garden. Miss Martha had said he was pruning back her prize bushes. It looked to Amanda like he was smoking a joint. It also appeared it was not his first.

"Hey, sweet stuff, how's it going?" he said from his comfortable position leaning against the huge trunk of a towering maple tree. There were a couple of dried-up rose petals in the vicinity that indicated he might have taken a single swipe at the bushes before taking his morning break.

"Is this what you're getting paid for?" Amanda inquired in her *sweet stuff* voice.

"Who are you, the garden club watchdog?"

"Nope, I'm just a reporter from *Inside Atlanta* with a few questions about what you might know about some items that are missing from homes where you work." She smiled to indicate just how friendly the questions were.

Dark, red-rimmed eyes instantly wary, Clement put out the joint and stuck it in his pocket. He got slowly to his feet. Muscles rippled, giving the impression that his sheer bulk alone had been responsible for ripping out the sleeves and stretching his T-shirt into its present ragged, body-hugging condition. "Lady, I got nothing to say to you."

"Why is that? Are you hiding something?"

"No, I'm not hiding anything, but I know my rights. I don't have to talk without a lawyer around."

"That's to cops. I'm a reporter. You get to talk to me all you want, especially if you're innocent."

"Innocent? I don't even know what the hell you're talking about. What's missing?"

"A gun, for one thing."

That seemed to drain the cocky attitude right out of him. He actually turned pale. He began patting his pockets and finally came up with a pack of ordinary, over-the-counter cigarettes. Camels, she noticed. She should have known. His hand shook as he lit one up.

"Hey, don't try to pin that on me," he said. "You get a gun, you're just asking for trouble. Why the devil would I steal one?"

"This one happened to be very valuable."

He blinked and tried to assimilate that bit of information. It seemed to be beyond him. "How come?"

"It was old." She took Larry's picture of the gun from her purse and showed it to him. "Ever seen one like it?"

"Nope. The kind of guns I see on the street don't look anything like that."

Amanda locked gazes with him. "Are you sure?"

He swallowed hard, then admitted, "I did see some fancy ones once in a case over at Miz Henderson's. She said they were her husband's collection. Is that where this one came from?"

Amanda decided that Clement Washington wasn't bright

enough to feign innocence that well. She stuffed the picture back into her purse. "No," she replied. "It was Miss Martha's. What about a Confederate flag? Have you seen one recently?"

"Stores all over have 'em."

"I mean an old one."

"Miz Taylor's got one over in Madison. Old Thomas, he told me all about it once."

"When was the last time you were over there?"

"The end of last week."

"Was the flag there then?"

"I guess so. I didn't really look at it. Why? Is that missing, too?"

Amanda nodded. "Where else do you work, Clement?"

"Here twice a week, Miz Taylor's, Miz Henderson's, and Miz Cosgrove's once a week. Sometimes, if Thomas needs me, I go back to Miz Taylor's on the weekend."

"Have you seen anyone hanging around over there or here that you didn't recognize?"

"Hell, I don't recognize none of these people. I didn't exactly grow up in their neighborhoods and most of their kids went to snooty private schools."

"How'd you get the jobs?"

"Miss Martha hired me on first. I came to the door one day and asked if she needed anybody."

"Who suggested you come here?"

"Nobody suggested it. I like working with plants and stuff. I was driving by and I saw that hers needed tending something fierce, so I took a chance. Up 'til then, I'd been working in a gas station. As soon as the old lady, I mean Miss Martha, as soon as she talked to her friends and got me those other jobs, I quit the gas station. She says she'll help me go to school and take horticulture next year. I ain't never had anybody take an interest in me like she has. She talks to me like I really matter. If anybody's bothering her, you just let me know about it. I'll take care of 'em.''

"No, Clement. The last thing Miss Martha would want would be for you to get yourself in trouble," Amanda said, revising her opinion of Clement Washington to one that was slightly more favorable. It was possible he was lying through his teeth, but if he was he was darned good at it. "You could keep an eye on things at all those houses, though. If you see anything odd, give me a call." She gave him her card. He tucked it in the same pocket with the joint, which gave her some hope that he'd run across it again.

"By the way," she added, "if you're so grateful to Miss Martha, you might try giving her a full day's work, instead of nodding off under the maple tree."

He regarded her nervously. "You're not going to tell her, are you? I mean about the joint. She's a lot like my grandma, only richer of course. She'd probably tan my hide if she found out."

Amanda laughed at the image that presented. Clement Washington was sixty or more years younger than Miss

Martha, twice her height, and double her weight. That wouldn't deter Miss Martha for a second.

"She probably would at that," Amanda concurred. She tapped him lightly on the shoulder. "It's something to keep in mind."

CHAPTER

Six

Amanda ate every last jelly bean in her purse en route back to the *Inside Atlanta* office. She figured she was going to need the energy if she was going to convince Oscar to hold that story on the historic homes for one more issue. He'd already postponed it once, when she'd gotten sidetracked by an investigation into the murder of a popular fitness instructor at an Atlanta health club. Oscar did not like changes in his schedules once they'd been posted and shuffled up to the publisher's office. Changes upset his monthly routines, which were so rigid they made military maneuvers seem lackadaisical.

"He's on the warpath," Jenny Lee Macon announced when Amanda walked through the reception area. There was no doubt at all that she was referring to Oscar. Amanda thought it was fitting that a "Sesame Street" grouch had been given the same name.

"Any particular reason?" she asked.

Jenny Lee ticked Oscar's entire repertoire off on her fingers. "It's nearly noon. You haven't called in since yesterday. He can't find the cover story on your desk. He doesn't know what he's paying you for, if you're not going to have your stories ready on time. Do you think this publication is an annual report? His ulcer's acting up and he's generally discontented with the human race. I think that about covers the top points."

Amanda laughed. "The usual."

"Yes, except for one thing."

"Which is?"

"He tried calling you at Donelli's."

"Oh," Amanda said softly.

Jenny Lee looked concerned. "Did you two break up? Oscar wouldn't say, but he looked really funny when he got off the phone, almost like you'd betrayed him."

It would be just like Oscar, Amanda thought, to take credit for her relationship with Donelli. The truth was he'd kicked and screamed every time he'd seen them together during the investigation into Chef Maurice's murder. He had not approved of his reporter and the chief cop on the case fraternizing. On an ethical level, neither had Amanda. It hadn't been her fault that the man was everywhere she turned. As for Donelli, if he'd had his way, he would have been the only one on the case, which would have solved the problem as he saw it. To his regret, Amanda had found his solution unacceptable.

"Well?" Jenny Lee prodded. "What happened with Joe?"

"We've had a slight disagreement." Amanda listened to the understatement pop out of her mouth and almost moaned. She was getting to be as bad as Miss Martha and the others.

"What about?"

One of the things Amanda had always admired about the receptionist was her persistence. It reminded her of herself when she was in hot pursuit of a story. This morning she found that she was less admiring than usual. "Let it go, Jenny Lee."

The girl looked chagrined. "Oh, sure. I didn't mean to pry. I just thought you might want to talk or something."

"Not about that. Not now, anyway."

Jenny Lee nodded so hard Amanda was sure it must be bad for her neck. "Okay," she said. "Got it. If you change your mind, though, I'm around. I know Larry's shoulder is there for you to cry on if you need it, too."

"Thanks, Jenny Lee. I'll remember that. Now I have to make a phone call. Tell Oscar I'll be in his office as soon as I've finished."

Jenny Lee looked nervous as she gazed past Amanda. "I don't think he wants to wait that long."

"Damn right, I don't," the editor in question bellowed from the doorway to the newsroom. "In my office, Amanda. Now!"

"It's so nice to see you this morning, too, Oscar," she said, rolling her eyes at Jenny Lee.

"Where have you been?" Oscar said when she was inside his office with the door shut. She was still standing right next to it, though, in case she decided she wanted to make a hasty exit.

"Working," she told him honestly.

He was shaking his balding head before she'd completed the second syllable of the word. "Not possible. Your assignment for today was to finish that story on the historic homes. Your computer is here. Your editor is here. The pictures are here. You, however, weren't here. I know you think the story is nothing but a piece of fluff, Amanda, but folks down here care about that sort of thing. I expect you to treat this assignment with the same respect you'd give to some big corruption scandal."

"Actually, that's what I'm trying to do. I had a last-minute interview."

"For this story?"

"Sort of."

"Either it was or it wasn't."

"I'll know better after I do some more digging." She tried to ignore Oscar's pained expression and took a deep breath. "I want to hold the story another month."

"You want to do what!" He loosened his tie, undid the

top button of his shirt, and ran his finger nervously around the inside of the collar. "Uh-uh. Forget it. We have a fortune invested in these pictures Larry shot. We have four pages in the middle of the magazine. We went through all of this last month."

"And I filled those pages with a damned good story, didn't I?"

"Okay, yes," he admitted with obvious reluctance. "It was a great story." His gaze narrowed thoughtfully. "You got something that good again?"

"Maybe."

"Oh, no. Not good enough. I can't fill the pages with maybes."

"Actually it's all part of the same story. Maybe if we just extended the deadline a week, maybe two, I could get what I need to flesh it out, fill in the gaps. I can't run with speculation and right now that's all I have. Trust me on this, Oscar. It could be big. Push the deadline just a little more for me. You could work it out with production."

"You know better, Amanda. I let you cut it right down to the wire with your deadlines as it is. I count on you being professional enough to meet them. We have distribution deadlines to worry about, advertising commitments to meet. The circulation department will go nuts if the next issue isn't out on time. It's a bad precedent for a new magazine. People start wondering what's going on if the next issue isn't on the stands when it's supposed to be. This venture gets labeled as a failure and we might as well pack it in. Rumor has a way of becoming fact. I can't just waltz up to Joel's office and say, oh, by the way, we're going to blow the production schedule all to hell because my star reporter had a hunch. You do have a hunch, don't you? That's what this is all about."

"It's more than a hunch."

He stopped pacing and stared at her. "You telling me you really do have something?"

"Yes. I'm just not sure what it is yet. I just know that we could look bad if we go with this before certain things are resolved."

"Explain, Amanda, and make it good. My stomach can't take this." He popped a handful of antacid tablets for emphasis. Amanda reached for her jelly beans before she realized that she'd eaten the last ones in her purse. She doubted if, in his present mood, Oscar would wait until she went to her desk for more. The desire for a chocolate jelly bean almost made her swoon with longing.

Since she was feeling desperate, she hurried through her explanation.

"Somebody snatched a multimillion-dollar gun from Miss Martha's. Now another Civil War treasure has been stolen from Ellie Mae Taylor. It puts a whole new perspective on the story if it involves some sort of sick conspiracy to drive these ladies nuts." When she was finished, Oscar simply stared at her. She could see him turning over in his mind everything she'd said. For all of his frustrating habits, he was a shrewd editor who didn't like getting beat on a story. He really hated being made to look like a fool.

"Okay, I hear what you're saying, but what do you think it means? What kind of conspiracy could it be? Who'd go after a bunch of sweet old ladies?"

Amanda sighed. "I don't know, but something weird is definitely going on. My gut instincts are never wrong, Oscar. You know that. I need more time to find out who's behind these thefts."

"Just this once couldn't you be satisfied to turn in a nice little feature without trying to make it into some big exposé?" he pleaded, but she could tell she had him on the hook. All she had to do was reel him in.

"I don't make the news," she reminded him. "I just report it."

"Yeah, right," he said, still sounding more skeptical than she would have liked. "What does Donelli think?"

Either Oscar really wanted the opinion of an ex-cop or he was fishing for her version of the status of her relationship. She had no intention of getting caught in the trap.

"We haven't discussed it," she said succinctly. "Now can I go call Willoughby's and see what they know about this? Miss Martha and her insurance agent are supposed to meet me here so we can make it a conference call. They should be in the lobby by now."

Oscar looked disappointed by his failure to get any insights into her personal life, but he nodded. "Go. As soon as you're finished with that, I want you back in here so we can think about this. Bring Miss Martha, if you want to. She's a sharp old gal. Maybe she'll have some ideas of her own. If the two of you can convince me that there's something to it, I'll see what I can do about buying us a couple of days."

Amanda groaned. "A couple of days!" she protested. "You know that's not long enough."

"That's the best we can hope for, Amanda. There's nothing we can use to fill that hole unless you want to dream up something overnight, research it, and get the pictures shot. There's not a free-lance story in the slush pile that I'd be willing to plug into a lead slot. Joel hired you to do those cover packages."

She scowled at the reminder and offered a suggestion edged in sarcasm. "Maybe you could do one of those photo spreads on Atlanta beauty queens you're always dreaming about. I'm sure Larry would be delighted to rush the assignment and Joel would be too busy asking for their phone numbers to complain too loudly."

"Just go make your call, Amanda. Meantime, I think I'll call Donelli and get him down here. We could . . ."

Her stomach turned over. She faced Oscar, leaned across his desk, and said distinctly, "Don't you dare."

He studied her expression, then sighed heavily. "Then I was right. You two did have a spat."

"We did not have a spat, as you call it."

"What then? Dammit, Amanda, how do you ever expect

to get married again if you keep giving the guy such a rough time?''

"Me? Me! Not that the issue of marriage is relevant in this case, but this wasn't my decision, Oscar Cates. It was Joe Donelli's. He walked out on me. Twice, as a matter of fact. Are you satisfied?''

Oscar looked shaken, torn between his loyalty to her and his respect for Donelli. He had actually invited Donelli to join in his weekly poker games. From what Amanda understood such invitations were harder to come by than country club memberships. Oscar coughed nervously and stared at the floor. He cleared his throat. Finally meeting her gaze again, he said reassuringly, "He'll be back, Amanda.'' If she'd been any closer, he probably would have poked her in the arm for added emphasis. Oscar's awkward attempt at comforting was so sweet it made her feel like crying.

She managed a jaunty smile that was one hundred percent bravado. "Who says I want him back," she said and left before Oscar could see the tears welling up in her eyes. She seemed to be making a lot of hurried, weepy departures these days. It was something she planned to hold against Donelli, if they ever got close enough again for him to notice that she was carrying a grudge.

Fortunately, there was no time at all for her to indulge in an extended bout of self-pity. Miss Martha and Graham Jenkins, her insurance agent, were waiting in the reception area. Miss Martha could hardly wait to get on the phone to the auction house. Mr. Jenkins seemed relieved by the discovery that he was here merely for corroboration and not to settle a multimillion-dollar claim.

When they finally reached Meredith Walters, the woman who was coordinating the November 2 auction, she listened to Amanda's explanation, then asked for verification to be sent at once. She gave them her fax number and Graham Jenkins went across the newsroom to send the papers.

"This doesn't make any sense. It's very rare that an item such as this would be consigned to auction under these circumstances," Ms. Walters continued in the meantime.

"Why?" Amanda asked. "Isn't that the way it would bring the most money?"

"Assuming that no one discovers that the object is stolen, but the risks are far too great for the professional thief. He knows that an item to be auctioned would be described and pictured in a catalog, which would then be circulated to any number of law enforcement agencies, including the FBI. It would also go to the International Association for Fine Arts Research, which keeps a record of stolen antiques and artworks. The odds of no one picking up on the fact that the item was stolen are slim."

Amanda exchanged a look with Miss Martha and suggested slowly, "Unless the thief counts on the fact that the victim won't report it."

"I suppose that's possible," Ms. Walters said. "Is that what happened in this instance?"

"It wasn't reported to official sources. Miss Wellington only informed her insurance company today in order to offer verification of ownership to you. There hasn't been any attempt to collect on her policy."

"I see."

"I assume you keep a record of the person offering the item to you for sale."

"Absolutely. In this instance, as I recall, it was a woman. One moment and I'll get the name."

Miss Martha's cane tapped impatiently as they waited. The sound, added to the prospect of bringing this case to a quick close, was beginning to make Amanda very anxious. She began popping jelly beans into her mouth in time to the staccato rhythm. She was surprised she didn't choke on them when Ms. Walters came back on the line and announced, "Well, I've found it, but I'm more confused than ever. According to our records, the woman who offered the gun for sale was a Miss Martha Wellington of Atlanta."

CHAPTER

Seven

"That is utterly absurd, young woman!" Miss Martha snapped at the Willoughby's representative, waving her cane threateningly in the direction of the speakerphone on Amanda's desk. She was obviously frustrated by not having a target she could see. "Describe this imposter, if you will."

"I'm very sorry, ma'am. I can't do that," Meredith Walters said, her voice amazingly steady considering the outburst her news had sparked.

"And why is that?" Miss Martha inquired tartly. "What sort of business do you people run up there?"

"Actually, that's the problem. The gun was consigned to our Atlanta office. If you'd care to go by there, perhaps

Mr. Davenport will be able to assist you. In the meantime, I will see that the item is withdrawn from the sale and returned to Atlanta at once. Rest assured, Miss Wellington, that we will be conducting our own investigation."

When Miss Martha reacted to this news with huffy silence, Amanda finally murmured their thanks and hung up.

Graham Jenkins scouted around the newsroom until he found some water, which he kept trying to get Miss Martha to sip. He was being so solicitous that Amanda wondered if he also carried the policies for Miss Martha's life insurance. Miss Martha kept pushing the water aside. When she looked as though she might clobber the officious Mr. Jenkins with her cane, Amanda stepped in and tried soothing her.

"Please, Miss Martha, you really mustn't get so excited. Your heart . . ."

Miss Martha's blue eyes turned on Amanda. They were glinting with indignation. "Let me worry about my heart, young lady. What do you expect me to do? Some horrible imposter is stealing my family heirlooms and running around using my name to sell them. Do you want me just to sit back and take it?"

"Of course not," Amanda said gently. "I think we should all go to the Willoughby's office and see what we can find out from this Mr. Davenport. I'm sure there's a very logical explanation."

Personally, Amanda couldn't imagine what it was unless

Miss Martha had taken leave of her senses or was selling off antiques in her sleep. She'd never seen any evidence that the elderly socialite and community historian was suffering from diminished mental capacity, but at eighty-two it was certainly possible.

Suddenly she recalled Deborah's comment about Mrs. Taylor. She had suggested that her employer's memory was getting fuzzy. Was there some sort of conspiracy at work to have all the old ladies in town declared mentally unfit? And why would anyone want to do that? Amanda was more convinced than ever that she was on to a fascinating angle that would make the piece on the historic homes into something with some real news impact and not just another routine feature.

First, though, she still had to have that meeting with Oscar to convince him that they were justified in holding the story back. She decided, however, that in her present state of agitation, Miss Martha should wait right where she was and calm down.

"Excuse me for just a minute, Miss Martha. I need to speak with Oscar and then we can go. You stay right here and relax."

But instead of remaining in Amanda's office, Miss Martha tap-tapped her way right down the hall behind her. Graham Jenkins was on her heels. When Amanda innocently led the parade into Oscar's office, he jumped up and yanked on his jacket. The action was so out of character, she couldn't imagine what had brought it on until she realized that he'd obviously glimpsed Miss Martha right behind her.

"Miss Wellington, it's a real pleasure to welcome you to *Inside Atlanta*," Oscar said formally, bowing over her hand. Miss Martha jerked her hand away impatiently and waved him off. Amanda watched the incident with open-mouthed astonishment. Oscar? Courtly? If she lived to be a hundred, she would never forget the moment she witnessed her irascible, unkempt boss turn into Rhett Butler.

"Young man," Miss Martha said in a tone that declared at once who was in charge. "Sit down." When Oscar was back behind his desk, she nodded in satisfaction. "Now, then. Let's get down to business. I need your assistance in a very grave matter, a matter of family honor. No, in fact, it's much more than that." She peered intently at him. "Can I count on you?"

Amanda had a hunch she could have gotten the loyalty of the marines with that softly drawled plea. Oscar was a snap. "Why, of course, Miss Martha," he said. "Anything we can do. You know that."

"Someone is out to get me," she announced as matter-of-factly as if she'd been listing the price of pole beans. "Amanda here seems to have a good head on her shoulders. She's proved that more than once, as I'm sure you're aware."

Oscar nodded obediently. Amanda began to enjoy the conversation. She even thought about hiring Miss Martha to work as her agent. If she could coerce Oscar into lending assistance this easily, perhaps she could manipulate an occasional salary increase and a few respectable bonuses for Amanda as well.

"I want you to loan her to me," Miss Martha declared.

Oscar and Amanda stared.

"Loan?" Amanda said.

"I'll pay you, dear. You don't have to worry about that. I just want you to finish what we've started here and I want your undivided attention while you're doing it. I don't want Oscar here to get it into his head that he can pull you to cover some inconsequential little story right in the midst of your investigation." There was the slightest hint of a twinkle in her eyes as she added, "I recall some of those scintillating pieces you had her do on the sewing club, Oscar Cates. A waste of talent, wouldn't you agree?"

Oscar looked as if he might explode, but he said docilely, "Absolutely. I wouldn't dream of doing that again, Miss Martha."

"He wouldn't," Amanda found herself agreeing hurriedly. She was so afraid of being turned over to Miss Martha lock, stock, and notebook that she was hardly able to enjoy the spectacle of Oscar's submissiveness. She decided she'd better assert herself now or wind up playing personal secretary, a role Miss Martha tended to cast her in all too often as it was. "Really, Miss Martha, Oscar will let me finish this story without interference, won't you, Oscar?"

"Well . . ."

"Oscar Cates . . ." Miss Martha began.

He closed his eyes for an instant, then sighed. "No, I won't interfere, but how long is this going to take?"

"There's no way of knowing that," Amanda admitted. "But I have a feeling it won't take all that long. With the information we got from that auction house a few minutes ago, we may even be able to wrap this up in a few hours, a couple of days at most."

"What did you find out?"

Amanda told him, with frequent outbursts of renewed indignation from Miss Martha.

Oscar nodded. "Okay. I suppose I can let you have a couple of days, but no longer, Amanda. Understand?"

"Absolutely."

Miss Martha bobbed her head in satisfaction. "Thank you, young man. You keep up the fine work, you hear. I'll tell your mama I saw you. She's a dear, sweet thing. You ought to drop by to visit her more often."

"Yes, ma'am," Oscar said.

"*Your mama?*" Amanda whispered in astonishment as she backed toward the door.

"Everybody has one, Amanda," Oscar growled, stripping off his jacket and tossing it over his chair. It fell, as usual, on the floor.

Biologically she accepted the necessity, but Oscar had always struck her as the sort of man who'd been sprung on the world fully grown. She'd always used that to account for his lack of manners. The morning had been full of surprises.

William Davenport III, the man in charge of Willoughby's South, was stuttering. As near as Amanda could tell, this was not his normal speech pattern. He sounded terrified. She peered through the open door to his understated but luxurious office and saw why at once. A tall, broad-shouldered man was leaning halfway across his desk. Under the right circumstances the posture might be considered friendly, even seductive. In this instance, it was clearly intimidating. She knew because the man was Donelli. She didn't wait for an invitation to join them.

Her entrance went unnoted by the panicky auction house manager. However, with the finely honed radar of an ex-cop or perhaps the antennae of a self-declared jilted lover, Donelli seemed to know the instant her foot crossed the threshold.

"It took you long enough," he said without turning around. "It's been a couple of hours since you got off the phone to Willoughby's."

Amanda didn't bother inquiring how he knew so much about her phone conversations. "I had a meeting with Oscar. What are you doing here?"

"I got a call a little while ago from New York. An old friend told me about a scam involving this gentleman and Miss Martha. Since I had my doubts about Miss Martha becoming involved in a conspiracy of this sort, I decided to get to know old William here.''

Amanda was impressed—and more than a little jealous. Donelli'd never jumped into a case just because she happened to mention it. If anything, quite the opposite. She began to wonder exactly what this Meredith Walters looked like and how friendly she and Donelli had been.

"What caught your interest?" she asked with genuine curiosity. "I've been talking about the same damned case for days now and it hasn't gotten you out of your bean patch."

He returned her look with a challenging gaze of his own. "Maybe you just didn't know the right buttons to push."

She swallowed hard at the jibe, but she refused to look away. "Maybe not," she said quietly. She wished desperately that Donelli would wrap his arms around her and apologize. She figured it was a long shot, especially with a roomful of interested spectators, so she pulled up a chair and sat down before she could make an utter fool of herself by throwing her arms around him.

William Davenport had taken the arrival of Amanda and Miss Martha as a good sign. The color had returned to his cheeks and he had pulled a comb out of the pocket of his dark gray suit and was carefully rearranging his few remaining strands of gray hair. As soon as he'd finished, he pushed the buzzer of his phone and suggested to someone that tea be served.

"How civilized," Donelli commented sarcastically. Mr.

Davenport turned pale again and began fussing with his gold cuff links.

"This is not a social call," Miss Martha concurred in a tone that was only slightly more polite. "I wish to know at once who has been here impersonating me."

Mr. Davenport's voice began low and skittered over a full octave as he repeated, "Impersonating you? I don't even know who you are, dear lady."

"Don't you *dear lady* me," Miss Martha snapped. She waved her cane threateningly. Amanda had seen her do it enough already this morning to move her chair well out of the way. This time, though, she was more interested in self-preservation than in protecting anyone else's hide. If Miss Martha happened to clip Mr. Davenport or Donelli, so much the better.

"You accepted property that belonged to me and sent it off for auction. Do you deny that?" Miss Martha demanded.

Davenport glanced at Donelli for help.

"The gun, William. Don't be obtuse."

"The Jefferson Davis gun belonged to you?" Mr. Davenport exclaimed nervously.

"I have the papers right here," Miss Martha said, pulling them from her purse. "If you need further proof, my insurance agent, Mr. Jenkins, will be more than happy to verify what I'm telling you." She gestured toward Jenkins who was hovering as far away from the reach of Miss Martha's cane as Amanda was.

"But I have the papers here," Mr. Davenport retorted, pulling a matching set from his file. "A Miss Martha Wellington brought the gun in for sale at the beginning of last week. All of the paperwork was in order. I went over it myself."

"Idiot!" Miss Martha declared, leaping to her feet and advancing on the hapless man. Donelli stopped her by taking her hand and patting it soothingly. It was just as effective on Miss Martha as it always had been on Amanda. She sank back into a chair next to Amanda's, picked up an advance copy of the auction catalog, and began fanning herself. When she realized what was pictured on page forty-seven, she dropped it as if she'd been scorched.

"You couldn't wait to get your cut, could you?" she said, advancing on Mr. Davenport again.

"Dear lady, please."

"Let's try a different approach," Donelli suggested gently, urging her back into her chair. "Mr. Davenport, have you and this lady ever met before?"

"No. Never." For all of his nervousness, Mr. Davenport looked as though he sincerely regretted his misfortune on that front.

"*This* is Miss Wellington."

"But that's not possible." He looked shaken.

"I assure you it is possible," Miss Martha said. "Any fool who's lived in Atlanta more than twenty minutes could testify to that."

Donelli ignored the sarcasm and persisted with his patient interrogation. "What did the woman who came to you look like?"

"She was younger, not young mind you, but in her sixties I'd say, maybe late fifties. Tall. Heavyset."

"Deborah," Amanda said thoughtfully as Miss Martha's head snapped around.

"Ellie Mae's Deborah?"

Amanda hadn't meant for her comment to be overheard. It reassured her that Miss Martha's hearing certainly wasn't impaired, no matter what the state of her mind might be. She only hoped Donelli hadn't been paying attention. She leaned closer to Miss Martha.

"Deborah certainly fits the description, don't you agree?"

"But she's never once been near my house, dear. I'm sure you must be mistaken."

"Are you certain she hasn't been there?"

"Never by invitation."

"That doesn't mean she doesn't know Della or that she hasn't slipped in on some pretext or other through the kitchen."

Miss Martha looked thoughtful. "I suppose not."

"Amanda, why on earth would you single out this Deborah person?" Donelli asked. He was obviously not above snooping on her private conversations. "Mr. Davenport's description could fit any number of women."

"Because . . . ." She wasn't so sure she wanted to share all of her guesswork with him until she fully understood his role in the investigation. "Whose side are you on, Donelli?"

"I am not on anyone's side, Amanda," he said in his most tolerant tone. "I'm just trying to get to the bottom of this."

"The bottom of what? The thefts? The fraud perpetrated against Willoughby's? Where exactly is your allegiance here?"

"Willoughby's is paying me, if that's what you're asking."

"It is, thank you very much." The clarification didn't exactly make her day. It tightened the ties between him and the mysterious Ms. Walters.

"Now will you answer my question?" he said. "Why do you suspect this Deborah?"

"Just because."

He gestured impatiently. "Dammit, Amanda. Are you going to let our personal differences keep us from working together on this?"

"We sure as hell didn't work together when we didn't have personal differences. Why should we change that now?"

Miss Martha was observing the bickering with keen interest. In fact, the last time Amanda had seen a glint like that in Miss Martha's eyes, she'd been trying to help Amanda and Mack patch up their differences. Her expression made Amanda very nervous.

"Amanda, dear, why don't you and Joseph go out for lunch and discuss this? Mr. Jenkins can give me a lift home and you and I can talk later."

Amanda scowled at Donelli, then said adamantly, "I do not want to go to lunch with *Joseph*. I have a job to do."

"Ditto," Donelli said, biting off the word as if he were just barely keeping his temper in check.

"But, dear, we are all on the same side, don't you see? It would be so much nicer if we all worked together."

"We are not on the same side," Amanda said. "I am an objective reporter. This is my story. He's a private investigator working for the auction house. He has a vested interest in how this turns out."

"All the same, I think it would be good if you talked. Now come along, both of you," she said in a tone Amanda normally heard used with small, petulant children. That tone and the fact that it might be deserved didn't improve her mood. Nor did Miss Martha's insistence.

"I'll take you all to lunch," she announced cheerfully when Amanda and Joe remained at a stalemate.

"Really, Miss Martha," Donelli objected, trying to back away. It was like trying to evade a steamroller. Miss Martha might be little, but she was definitely mighty when her mind was made up.

Miss Martha linked her arm through his before he could complete the thought or the retreat. She waved a beckoning hand at Mr. Davenport. "You, too, William. Graham.

Come along. We might as well all go. Five heads will be better than two, no doubt.''

"Especially if two of them aren't speaking," Amanda grumbled, but she joined the procession. If there was going to be a conversation that might be relevant to this story, she was not going to be the only one not in on it.

CHAPTER
Eight

The restaurant Miss Martha chose was a tearoom, where she was clearly well known and apparently held a standing reservation. The maître d' ushered them to her "usual" table, which had a view of all proceedings and an entire stable of eager waiters hovering nearby. Water glasses were filled before they could even reach for their linen napkins. Amanda fully expected lunch to appear before they could open their menus. From the solicitous service to the understated but definitely feminine decor, the tearoom was designed to attract Atlanta's loveliest, wealthiest belles. It was not meant for Donelli.

To Amanda's amusement he looked around at all the pink flowered chintz and French provincial furniture and practically turned pale. Once they'd been given menus, she almost laughed aloud at his attempts to locate a hamburger or even spaghetti on a menu that was predominated by dainty tea sandwiches and slenderizing fruit plates. The closest he could come was a seafood pasta salad. His expression was sour as he placed the order. When William Davenport, obviously feeling that the worst of the crisis over the gun had passed, enthusiastically declared he'd have the same, Donelli looked as though he wanted to cancel and stick to black coffee.

"Now, then," Miss Martha said, beaming at them. "Isn't this lovely?"

"Lovely," Mr. Davenport concurred.

"Just perfect," Graham Jenkins agreed.

Amanda nodded politely. Donelli scowled.

"Miss Martha, I really do think you ought to let me call the senator," Graham Jenkins said. "He would want to know about what's been happening."

"There is no need to involve my nephew in this. I'm sure he's much too busy in Washington to worry himself over something I am perfectly capable of handling."

"But Miss Martha . . ."

She tapped her cane emphatically. "Enough, Graham. I will take care of this."

On the surface, the insurance agent accepted the rebuke calmly enough, but it appeared to Amanda that he was seething underneath. No one seemed to know quite what to say to smooth things over. Not even Miss Martha's expertise as a hostess could keep the conversation afloat.

When Mr. Davenport launched into a tedious discussion of an upcoming auction of snuffboxes, Amanda dropped all pretense of listening. She began mentally sorting through the information she had. It wasn't all that much. She couldn't even prove for certain that the theft of Mrs. Taylor's flag was linked to the disappearance of Miss Martha's Jefferson Davis gun.

Unless, she corrected, she could prove that Deborah had the opportunity to take the gun. If Mr. Davenport also identified Deborah as the woman who brought him the gun, then it stood to reason she was behind the theft of the flag as well. But why? Amanda could understand Deborah stealing the flag just to drive Mrs. Taylor nuts, but what did she have against Miss Martha? Or had she stolen the gun because of the millions of dollars it might bring at auction? But how would she have even known something like that? Deborah didn't strike her as someone who'd be educated in the value of antique pistols. Amanda's head was spinning with the possibilities, none of which made a bit of sense.

"Donelli," she began thoughtfully, before his startled expression reminded her that they weren't speaking. "Never mind."

"What, Amanda?"

"Nothing."

"Go ahead, dear," Miss Martha encouraged, watching the two of them expectantly.

"I just wanted him to pass the salt."

Donelli shook his head at the ridiculous fib and pointed at the little silver shaker sitting right in front of her.

"Oh."

"Indeed."

At least he hadn't mentioned that there wasn't a single thing on her plate requiring salt. "You don't have to be so smug," she muttered.

"All ex-cops are smug. It's one of our nicer and more deserved traits. We know so much."

"You don't know everything."

"I know quite a lot. I know, for instance, that it is driving you crazy to think that I might actually beat you on this case. You liked it a whole lot better when I was just trailing along after you trying to keep you from getting killed."

Amanda couldn't believe her ears. "That is not true. I've been pleading with you for months to get back into police work again."

"What you really want is for me to be in a position to feed you information."

"That is not what I want. I just want you to be happy."

"As long as it doesn't pit us against each other, right?"

"Are we against each other, Joe?" she said softly, ignoring the presence of the others. "Was I right about that?" Suddenly, it seemed very important to find out exactly where things stood between them, if the relationship had deteriorated so badly that they couldn't even work side by side.

He frowned. "I didn't mean it that way."

She sighed regretfully. "I think you did," she said, pushing away her plate of cute little triangle-shaped chicken salad and egg salad sandwiches.

He reached over and put his hand over hers. She sensed the apology behind the cautious touch. She wanted to curl her fingers around his and hang on. She didn't.

"I just meant that you're very competitive," he said with a sigh. "It wasn't personal."

"How can it not be personal when it's between you and me?"

"Oh, for heaven's sake, Amanda," he said impatiently, dropping his napkin over the seafood pasta as if he couldn't wait to hide it from sight. He noted the interested gazes of Miss Martha and Mr. Davenport and added pointedly, "This is not the time or the place for us to be wrangling about our personal differences."

His gaze collided with hers, skittered away, then came back to stay. Her heart flipped over obediently. Amanda was so busy staring into those soulful brown eyes of his that she didn't notice the arrival of Mack until Miss Martha exclaimed cheerfully, "Why, Mack, dear, I'm so glad you could join me. This is turning into a wonderful party."

Dismayed, Amanda stared at her ex-husband, who seemed delighted to find her there. He patted her on the shoulder then allowed his hand to linger possessively as he was introduced to the others. Amanda watched Donelli, who looked as though he'd been stabbed in the back. The tension at the table was so thick a Cuisinart couldn't have cut through it.

Amanda glowered at Miss Martha. She had had about all of her meddling she could stand. "You asked him here?" she said so coldly that Mack's hand finally fell away.

Miss Martha didn't seem the least bit perturbed by Amanda's irritation or the uncomfortable tension she'd created. "I asked him before I knew that the rest of you would be joining me," she explained. "But it's all working out ever so nicely, don't you think? We can all have a nice chat about this awful conspiracy. Sit down, Mack. I'm sure the maître d' can bring over another chair."

"There's no need," Donelli said, shoving his chair back so hard it almost slid into the next table. "I'm just leaving."

Amanda watched him stand up, listened to his polite but insincere thanks to Miss Martha for the interesting lunch, and followed his awkward maneuvering through the narrow aisles meant for more petite figures. Glaring once more at Miss Martha, she jumped up just as Donelli reached the door and ran after him.

"You are not going anywhere without me," she announced.

"We're on opposite sides, isn't that what you told me just minutes ago? Why should you want to come with me?" Donelli asked.

"That's precisely why. I need to keep an eye on you so I'll know what you're up to."

"Still afraid I'll come up with a lead you'll miss, Amanda?"

"No, I'm afraid you'll blunder around and mess things up for me," she said nastily. She had lost patience with his taunts, with Miss Martha's interference, and pretty much with the world in general.

Donelli feigned an offended expression. "I do not *blunder around*, as you so sweetly put it. I investigate. Trial and error, one little lead at a time."

"You used to investigate like that. Now you farm," she reminded him, running to keep up with him. "Where are you going right now?"

"To see this Deborah person you mentioned."

"There," she said triumphantly. "That's exactly what I meant. You don't even know who she is."

"I may not know her last name, but I do know where to find her. Hundreds of cases have been solved on slimmer leads than that."

"I don't suppose I can stop you."

"Not a chance. Willoughby's is paying me very well to discover who tried to defraud them. Selling stolen goods is very bad for their stodgy reputation."

"I suppose this Meredith Walters person asked you as a personal favor."

"Something like that."

The response did not gladden her heart. She studied his intractable expression and recognized the futility of arguing. "Okay, let's go."

There was a definite touch of irony lurking in his grin. "How wonderful that you can join me."

"I knew you'd be thrilled."

"Shall I drive?"

"I wouldn't have it any other way," she mumbled, regretting more than anything that she'd left her car at the office. Donelli drove the way he investigated, with plodding patience. It drove her nuts under the best of circumstances. Considering how well they were getting along at the moment, this was not the best of circumstances. If he turned on his favorite country music station, there was a very good chance that she might commit mayhem.

"Mind a little music?" he asked right on cue.

She glowered at him and started digging frantically in her purse for soothing ice blue mint jelly beans. There wasn't even a licorice one lingering with the lint in a corner. She swore under her breath.

"We'll compromise," he said, clearly interpreting her deteriorating mood. There was a definite twinkle in his eyes as he suggested, "How about easy listening?"

The music would sooner soothe a savage beast than it would her frazzled nerves, but Amanda nodded. "Fine."

"Want a stick of gum?"

"No."

"Suit yourself," he said, unwrapping one and popping it into his mouth. She could practically taste the peppermint. She refused, though, to ask for any. She bit down on her lower lip and stared straight ahead.

When they'd left the outskirts of Atlanta behind en route to Madison, Amanda sneaked a look at Donelli. He was frowning again. Either he was thinking very hard about the case or he was still in a snit over Mack's arrival at the restaurant.

"Joe, why did you leave the minute Mack showed up back there?"

He turned an incredulous gaze on her, shook his head, and turned back to stare at the highway. "Call me crazy, Amanda, but I wasn't much in the mood to sit around exchanging small talk with your ex-husband. Maybe in Hollywood ex-husbands and lovers can all pal around together, but I'm not that sophisticated."

"You barely said hello to the man. Couldn't you have put your personal feelings aside for just a minute? He might have been able to help us think through what's been happening. He was the one who discovered the Willoughby's connection, after all."

"If you wanted to chat with him, you were perfectly free to stick around."

"I had to follow you."

"You didn't have to. You're a free agent. You can hang out with any man you choose."

"That's not what I meant and you know it."

"Would you have stayed if you'd thought I was just going off to pick up groceries?"

She understood all too clearly the point he was getting at. She pondered the question for several minutes before finally admitting, "I honestly don't know anymore."

Donelli sighed. "*That's* what I meant."

"I'm sorry," she said.

"You don't have to be sorry. I'm the one who pointed out that you weren't over the man, remember? I shouldn't have asked the question if I wasn't prepared for the answer."

"I hate this."

He took one hand off the steering wheel and rubbed away yet another stupid tear that was making its way down her cheek.

"So do I, Amanda," he said wearily. "So do I."

Deborah did not exactly throw out the welcome mat when they arrived on the Taylor doorstep in Madison. She scowled at Amanda, then looked Donelli up and down as if she wanted to determine whether she should go back inside and lock up the silver.

"Mrs. Taylor's gone out," she muttered, still bracing the door as if she feared they might try to overrun her to gain entry.

"That's okay," Amanda said. "We really wanted to talk with you."

"What about?"

"Couldn't we come in for a minute? It won't take long," Donelli promised, smiling at the housekeeper. That smile had won over tougher customers than Deborah. She still looked suspicious, but she stepped back and held open the door.

"I suppose it can't hurt nothing," she said grudgingly. "You'll have to come to the kitchen, though. I'm baking pies."

They followed her through the house. In the warm kitchen, which was fragrant with the scent of apples and cinnamon and fresh brewed coffee, she gestured toward the chairs drawn up to a round oak table.

"You want some coffee?" she asked, her years of training overcoming her natural suspicion.

"I'd love some," Donelli said, smiling again. This time Deborah's lips actually twitched as if she were trying to smile back. Amanda watched what was for Deborah almost flirtatious byplay in astonishment.

"Nothing smells better than a kitchen where something's baking," he added, sniffing appreciatively.

The last of Deborah's reserve crumbled. "I just took one pie out of the oven. You want a piece of that?" she asked Donelli, pointedly excluding Amanda.

"If you're sure it's okay," he told her, "I'd love a piece. Wouldn't you, Amanda?"

"Sure," she murmured. Deborah probably couldn't slip in any arsenic with the two of them in plain sight.

When the coffee and pie had been served—her slice was about a third the size of Donelli's generous slab—Donelli addressed Deborah. "When Mrs. Taylor goes to visit her friends, do you ever go along with her?" he inquired. "Great pie, by the way."

"Thank you and no, I do not go with her. I ain't no lady's companion. I'm the housekeeper. Have been for nigh on to thirty years, I reckon. I was here long before *she* was."

"But in all that time, surely you've met some of Mrs. Taylor's friends, been to their homes."

"Not that I recall. Oh, I've met 'em, but I don't hobnob with 'em, if you know what I mean."

"What about here? Do any of her friends ever bring their housekeepers along when they come to visit here?"

Deborah regarded them suspiciously again. "Look, it's clear enough this ain't no social call. Why don't you just come out and ask whatever's on your mind?"

"Have you ever been to Miss Martha Wellington's home?" Amanda asked bluntly, slipping into her bad cop demeanor, since Donelli had obviously cast himself in the role of friendly cop.

Deborah shook her head. "Never."

"Do you know Della, Miss Martha's housekeeper?"

"No. Now suppose you two tell me what this is all about?" she inquired with icy insistence.

"My guess is that they're trying to pin the theft of Miss

Martha's Civil War heirloom on you, Deborah," said a cheerful voice from the doorway.

Deborah gasped indignantly and picked up her rolling pin. Amanda whirled around for a look at the man who'd spoken. Donelli, she noted, didn't seem surprised by the intrusion. His sixth sense again. He ignored Deborah's raised rolling pin, glanced casually over his shoulder, and inquired with lazy interest, "Who are you?"

The man stiffened. He didn't look like the type who was used to being questioned. "Might I ask the same thing? You are, after all, in my home."

Donelli introduced himself and Amanda, then said pointedly, "Your turn."

"I'm Henry Taylor. I just stopped by to visit my stepmother."

"She's out," Deborah said, energetically slamming the rolling pin into a mound of pie crust dough. She rolled the dough out with short, agitated strokes. She didn't look up from the counter.

Amanda watched the housekeeper closely. Henry Taylor's arrival seemed to make her even more nervous than she had been. Since there didn't seem to be a lot more they could learn from her under the present circumstances, Amanda suggested, "Why don't we go into the living room and get acquainted, Mr. Taylor? I've heard quite a lot about you from your stepmother."

"I believe she's mentioned you, as well, Miss Roberts, though I don't recall hearing any mention of Mr. Donelli.''

"We haven't met," Donelli said, not bothering to explain further.

"I see. Well, come along then. I suppose I can spare a few moments. Bring your coffee and pie along if you like.''

"That's not necessary," Amanda said. "We were finished.''

Donelli glared at her and looked regretfully at the remaining pie on his plate. Deborah did not offer to wrap it up for him, indicating just how cowed she was by Henry Taylor or how badly Donelli had slipped in her estimation.

In the living room—Amanda noted with interest that he did not take them into the less formal parlor where she'd met with Mrs. Taylor—Henry gestured for them to be seated. He remained standing, his elbow propped on the fireplace mantel. With his polished Italian shoes, custom-tailored suit, monogrammed shirt, silk tie, and Rolex watch, he was the epitome of a modern, Southern gentleman of means. That his pose was reminiscent of portraits from another era was probably not something he intended, Amanda decided—unless he was hoping she'd call Larry back in for another shot for the upcoming feature layout in *Inside Atlanta*. She could just see the caption: TAYLOR FAMILY SCION AT HOME IN 19TH-CENTURY MANSION.

"Why were you questioning Deborah?" he inquired.

"I thought you already had the answer to that," Donelli commented.

Henry Taylor looked shaken by the direct response. "You really were trying to pin that theft on her?"

"Let's just say some questions have arisen that might tend to incriminate her."

Henry began pacing. "Oh, dear, that's not good, not good at all. Mother will be distraught."

"I doubt it," Amanda murmured.

Two pairs of quizzical male eyes turned on her. "Nothing," she said. "Tell me, Mr. Taylor, are you aware that your stepmother's Confederate flag was stolen sometime in the last few weeks?"

"Stolen? Don't be ridiculous. Who would steal it?"

"It is valuable."

"The market, however, is very narrow. It seems unlikely that someone would waste his time trying to track down a buyer when there are so many other more valuable things in the house to take, items that would arouse no particular curiosity on the part of the buyer."

"That bothered me, too, at first," Amanda conceded. "Now I'm not so sure. If the same person who stole Miss Martha's gun also took the flag, then they know all about the market for Civil War memorabilia. You, in fact, seem to know quite a lot about this market. Why is that?"

"It is virtually impossible to live in this town and not have a nodding acquaintance with Civil War antiques and anecdotes. This is, after all, the place that General Sherman found too beautiful to burn, according to the legend. Let me assure you, though, you're making much too much of this missing flag. Unfortunately, my stepmother's mind has been a little hazy recently. I'm sure she simply sent the flag out for cleaning and forgot about it. No doubt it will turn up in a few days and that will be the end of that.''

"Deborah suggested the same thing when I was here the other day. I see no evidence that your stepmother's memory is at all diminished. She's also checked with her handyman. He never sent the flag to be cleaned. Nor did his helper touch it. I've talked to him myself. Do you suppose Mrs. Taylor climbed a ladder and took it down herself?'' Amanda asked innocently.

Henry Taylor smiled back just as guilelessly. "She wouldn't have to climb a ladder, Miss Roberts. There's a perfectly adequate mechanism for raising and lowering the flag. It requires neither strength nor ingenuity.''

Amanda's spirits sagged. "I see.''

"Now, if you two will excuse me, I must be getting back to work. I'll walk you out.''

Since he didn't seem to be leaving them with any alternative, they went with him. When he'd driven away in his Cadillac, Amanda turned to Donelli, who was staring after the sleek gray car. It was so new it still had the temporary registration tag in the back window.

"What'd you think?'' she said.

"I'm not crazy about the way he talked about his stepmother," he admitted. "But that's not grounds for accusing him of anything except insensitivity."

"You know what I don't get? It seems to me like everyone is trying very hard to set this up to look as though those two women are addlepated."

"I know. That's the way it seems to me, too. Any idea why?"

"One thing crosses my mind. What if Henry Taylor's trying to have his stepmother declared mentally incompetent, so he can take over management of the estate?"

"Any indication that he's doing that?"

"I don't know. She seems to think he's the kindest, most generous man ever to walk the face of the earth. She already relies on him quite a bit. I wonder what Oscar knows about him? He knows everyone there is to know in these parts. He lived in Morgan County most of his life."

"Let's go talk to Oscar, then."

Donelli's automatic assumption that he was to be included in the conversation with Oscar grated on Amanda's nerves. It was her own fault, of course. Over the last year or so, she had gotten into the habit of bouncing ideas around with Donelli. Just now she'd been so busy speculating aloud that she hadn't thought about how much of her own plan she was divulging to the competition.

When they got off the elevator in the *Inside Atlanta* reception area, Jenny Lee's face lit up at the sight of them together.

"Oh, Amanda, honey, I'm so . . ."

"Save it, Jenny Lee," Amanda ordered before Jenny Lee gushed out something embarrassing. "Is Oscar in?"

"He sure is and he's been busting a gut looking for you. He's gonna be real excited to see you're back." She beamed at Donelli. "You, too."

"Why me, too?" Joe muttered as he followed Amanda across the newsroom.

"You don't want to know."

"Yes, I do."

"Take it from me," she insisted. "You don't."

Oscar came barreling out of his office just then and met them halfway across the room. He, too, was beaming. Apparently Jenny Lee had wasted no time in spreading the news that Amanda was back with Donelli in tow. "Joe, how are you?" he said, pumping Donelli's hand as if he hadn't seen him in years.

Donelli cast another helpless look at Amanda.

"Come right in," Oscar said. "It's good to see you two working together. Just like old times, right, Joe?"

"Like old times," Donelli concurred with a wry look at Amanda. She shrugged.

Oscar caught the exchange and tempered his enthusiasm. "I'm glad you finally got back here, Amanda. Mrs. Cosgrove has been calling here for the last two hours. She won't talk to anyone but you."

"Henrietta Cosgrove?" Donelli asked. "The woman whose family owns half the real estate in Madison?"

"She's the one," Amanda said.

"How do you know her?"

She wasn't wild about his incredulous tone, but she responded just the same. "I interviewed her for the piece I'm writing on historic homes. Maybe she's thought of something more for the article."

"I doubt it," Oscar said. "Sounded to me like she was about to bust a gusset over something."

"I'll call right now, then."

"You can do it from here," Oscar offered.

Amanda looked at him, glanced at Donelli, and shook her head. "I'll call from my desk, so you two can catch up on old times."

Donelli chuckled at her obvious ploy. "Your generosity will be duly noted, Amanda. Just don't try sneaking out the back way."

"I wouldn't dream of it," she replied as Oscar regarded them both curiously. He appeared to be speculating on the odds that they'd both taken leave of their senses.

Which, she noted as she went to her desk, was entirely possible. How could two people who'd been so happy only a few weeks ago manage to mess things up so badly? There wasn't time to figure that out as she flipped through her card file until she found Mrs. Cosgrove's unlisted number, so she put it on a back burner until she had some time to ponder it in depth.

"Amanda, thank goodness you called," Mrs. Cosgrove exclaimed at once. Oscar was right, she did sound agitated.

"What is it? Is something wrong?"

"Wrong? I'll say it is. Do you remember that lovely watch I showed you? The one that was stolen by General Sherman's soldiers, but eventually returned to my great grandmother."

"Yes. What about it?"

"It's gone."

"Gone?" Amanda repeated weakly. Not again.

"Are you deaf, dear? The watch has been stolen. I know I should have looked right away after what happened to Miss Martha and Ellie Mae, but I didn't. You must come over here at once. I want to know what you're going to do about it," she declared imperiously.

The phone clicked off and Amanda was left listening to a dial tone. Something in Mrs. Cosgrove's statement worried her even more than the announcement that yet another expensive heirloom was missing.

"I want to know what you're going to do about it."

That was it, all right. Mrs. Cosgrove was laying this one at her feet. Somewhere along the line all the dear little old ladies of the historical society had gotten the notion that she was a private eye. Worse, she had a horrible feeling that she'd promoted just that misconception with her repeated references to herself as an investigative reporter. Obviously, they didn't fully understand the fine distinction between the two occupations.

"So, what's she all worked up about?" Donelli asked, coming up behind her.

"There's been another theft."

"Another one?" Oscar said. "I don't like this, Amanda. I don't like it one bit."

"These ladies aren't too crazy about it either, Oscar, but you have to admit the story is getting more and more interesting."

"Well, what are you doing about figuring out what's behind the thefts?"

"Me? I'm just reporting the damned story," she said, admittedly touchy about everyone's assumption that she was the journalistic equivalent of Sherlock Holmes.

Donelli hooted at her response.

"What's so funny?" she demanded.

"I'll remind you of that the next time you're inclined to stick your nose in where it doesn't belong."

"Go to hell, Donelli," she snapped, grabbing up her purse, dumping in a handful of jelly beans, and stalking off. Halfway across the newsroom she turned around and said, "Well, are you coming or not?"

"Where are you going?" Donelli inquired as he joined her.

"Where else? To stick my nose in where it doesn't belong."

CHAPTER

Nine

Amanda drove. She wasn't sure she could endure riding in Donelli's decrepit old Chevy at thirty-five miles an hour clear to Madison twice in one day. Donelli flinched when she lurched from the parking garage into bumper-to-bumper downtown Atlanta rush-hour traffic with barely an inch to spare. He seemed almost relieved when she reached the highway and accelerated to within what she considered a perfectly safe five miles an hour above the posted limit.

"You don't suppose this thing with the watch is a co-incidence?" she said, weaving neatly between cars.

"Do you?" He gripped the seat with white-knuckled determination as she made a tight cut back into the right-hand lane.

"No," she admitted. "I was just hoping you would.

-133-

Something about all of this really bothers me. I can deal with a nice, clear-cut murder, but this seems so devious. I can't begin to figure out what the thief is hoping to accomplish.''

"Maybe he wants what any thief wants: money."

"I don't think so. Then what Henry Taylor says would make more sense. He'd take something easier to fence. This thief is being very particular. Do you know if any other Civil War memorabilia has turned up at Willoughby's?''

"None, at least not from the Atlanta area. I called Meredith from Oscar's office. They got in one item last week, a Confederate uniform cape I think she said, but it came from someplace in Maryland. She's already checked to make sure it came in legitimately.''

"And?''

"It had. She spoke to the man selling it. It belonged to his great-great uncle. It's been moldering in his attic for the past hundred years or so.''

"Sounds attractive.''

"Meredith was excited.''

Amanda scowled. She wasn't overly interested in Meredith Walters's state of mind. It irritated her that Donelli seemed to be. "Did you get a chance to ask Oscar about Henry Taylor?''

"Yes. He says Henry Senior was a financial genius. He started the family banking empire, built it up over his lifetime and turned it over to Henry about ten years ago.

Up until he died, though, he still ran things, even though Henry Junior had the title of president.''

"I wonder how come. Couldn't he let go?"

"Either that or he was worried about how his son was handling responsibility.''

"Did Oscar have any idea what Henry's present financial status is?''

"Nope. He did say that Taylor has his own place in Buckhead in Atlanta. Quite a mansion from what he hears, even more impressive than the old family estate in Madison. He must be doing just fine.''

"Any children?''

"A couple of daughters. Oscar thinks they're both away at some fancy women's college in New England, much to his stepmother's dismay. Apparently she was appalled that the girls would be sent to a Yankee school.''

"I can imagine," Amanda said. "I think she, Miss Martha, and Mrs. Cosgrove all went to school in Virginia. They seem to have very definite ideas about proper upbringing for young ladies. I'm pretty sure she favors piano lessons over political science. I don't know about those schools, but the Ivy League colleges all cost a fortune. Could Henry Junior be strapped for cash because of that?''

"Oscar says he was boasting all over that they'd both won academic scholarships. Even if it didn't pay the full freight, it should have kept him out of hock.''

Amanda added up the information from several different directions and still couldn't come up with a logical total that would implicate Henry Taylor, at least not beyond the reasonable doubt required by law. "You don't suppose he really is just worried about his stepmother's mental lapses, do you?"

"I guess we'll know if that Confederate flag turns up in a hall closet or something."

"But even that wouldn't explain away Miss Martha's gun or Mrs. Cosgrove's pocket watch."

"Well, now's our chance to find out more about the watch, anyway," Donelli said as Amanda pulled into the circular driveway in front of Mrs. Cosgrove's huge antebellum home just off Old Post Road.

Built of old brick in 1857, it was trimmed with white shutters. Intricate ironwork decorated the veranda and a magnificent magnolia tree, its pink waxy blooms now fallen, shaded the front yard. Inside, many of the rooms had fireplaces. The wide plank floors gleamed and the windows sparkled. The huge old place with its half dozen bedrooms upstairs was far too large for an elderly widow living alone. Amanda had noticed during her interview that Mrs. Cosgrove apparently lived in the downstairs rooms and kept the upstairs closed off except when the house was open for tours. She was waiting at the door for them now, looking every bit as if she were planning to give them a guided trip through her showcase home.

Henrietta Cosgrove was tall, reed thin, and wore her white hair swept up in an old-fashioned cluster of curls on top of her head. Every curl was in place, but her frameless reading glasses had slipped to the end of her nose. She peered at Amanda with clear turquoise eyes that sparkled with intelligence.

"Who's he?" she said, glancing appraisingly at Donelli.

"This is Joe Donelli, Mrs. Cosgrove. He's a private investigator who's been looking into what happened over at Miss Martha's a few weeks ago. He came along since we thought this might be related."

She nodded and ushered them down the long, wide foyer to a parlor where a fire blazed in the grate, though it was only pleasantly cool outdoors. "I get chilled easily," Mrs. Cosgrove said, wrapping a lacy web of fine blue wool more tightly around her silk-clad shoulders. "If you'll be uncomfortable in here, we could go into the other room."

"No, this is just fine," Amanda said, sitting down on one of the overstuffed chairs that faced the fire. Mrs. Cosgrove sat across from her. Donelli was relegated to standing—or sitting on a footstool. Amanda hoped like crazy that he'd opt for the stool, preferably at her feet. Naturally he didn't. He paced as she asked, "When exactly did you discover that the watch was missing, Mrs. Cosgrove?"

"Just this morning. I went to the cabinet to dust and it wasn't there. The cabinet was locked up just the way it always is. There was no indication that anyone had tampered with the lock. But the watch was missing just the same."

"Why were you doing the dusting?" Donelli asked.

Mrs. Cosgrove stared at him. "Just who else was going to do it, young man?" Her chin rose just a notch to a proud, defiant angle.

Amanda caught the embarrassment in Donelli's eyes. "Sorry. I just assumed you had someone to help."

"I do have a girl who comes in once a week to do the heavy cleaning that I can't manage, but I do the rest. It's a waste of good money to pay someone to do things I can perfectly well do myself. Besides, I wouldn't trust anyone else to dust this particular cabinet."

"When was the last time you dusted?"

She looked embarrassed. "I don't remember exactly. Two, maybe three weeks ago. I haven't felt all that well lately."

"It's always kept locked?"

"Always."

"Does your girl know where the key is kept?"

"I may be old, Mr. Donelli, but I am hardly senile. What would be the point of keeping it locked if half the world knew the whereabouts of the key?"

Donelli grinned. "You have a point. Could I see the cabinet?"

"Do you promise not to peek when I get the key from its hiding place?" she asked and Amanda caught the quick glimmer of amusement in her eyes.

"On my honor," he said solemnly. Amanda choked back a sarcastic comment. Donelli turned and glared at her.

Mrs. Cosgrove led them into the living room where the large, glass-fronted display case occupied a good portion of one wall. She left them alone while she went after the well-protected key. While she was gone, Amanda recalled Mrs. Cosgrove's evident pride as she'd pointed out the various treasures inside. Donelli, however, was less interested in the contents than he was in the lock.

"I'd give anything to have this glass dusted for prints," he said.

Mrs. Cosgrove overheard him. "I will not have the police stomping through here making a mess of things," she said sternly, making it clear that that was that. "I'm sure you and Miss Roberts are perfectly capable of tracking down the thief. If Miss Martha is paying you, Mr. Donelli, I'd be happy to match your fee."

"That won't be necessary, Mrs. Cosgrove. The auction house is paying me plenty." He leaned down to examine the brass keyhole more closely. "No sign of any tampering. You have a sharp eye, Mrs. Cosgrove. Has there ever been a duplicate key for the cabinet?"

"Never."

"When did you last open it?"

She looked thoughtful. "Why, I expect it was the day I showed the items to Amanda and that photographer. What was his name, dear?"

"Larry Carter."

"Of course. I remember. I don't believe he came from around here originally or I would have recalled his grandparents." She said it as though he'd committed a crime, but moderated the criticism by adding, "A very polite young man. He asked if we could open the doors so his flash wouldn't reflect on the glass and cause a glare. I was most happy to oblige. I do like sharing my treasures with the public whenever I can. That's why I continue to participate in the home tours, even though it's a lot of extra work."

"So all sorts of people know about the pocket watch and your other heirlooms," Donelli said.

"Certainly. I suppose everyone in Madison has seen them at one time or another."

"That certainly narrows things down," Amanda said dryly.

"Don't get discouraged, Amanda. We've barely gotten started," Donelli reminded her. "There are all sorts of angles we haven't checked yet."

Though it was directed at her, Amanda wasn't sure whether the remark was really made for her benefit or Mrs. Cosgrove's. She assumed it was for the elderly widow's, since she knew better. They had no suspects. They didn't even have a decent lead or a plausible motive.

"Mrs. Cosgrove, do you know Henry Taylor?" she asked for lack of anything better to pursue, while Donelli wandered around poking into corners, looking for who knows what.

"Of course, dear, why would you ask?"

"What's his relationship been like with his step-mother?"

"With Ellie Mae? Why, it seems to me they've always gotten along rather well under the circumstances."

"What circumstances?" Amanda asked.

"He could have been put out when he discovered that his daddy was leaving her most of his assets, along with a say in how the banks were to be operated, but young Henry took it just fine."

Donelli's head snapped around at that. "Mrs. Taylor has control over the banks?"

Mrs. Cosgrove nodded. "I don't know if you'd call it control, but she does have a seat on the board. Ellie Mae of all people." She clucked her tongue disapprovingly, then added, "Seems to me like a waste. I don't know that she's ever exercised her voting privileges. As dear as she is, Ellie Mae just doesn't have much of a head for business. She's always been content to let Henry Junior vote her proxy, as far as I know. Still and all, she could put a monkey wrench in things, if she was ever of a mind to."

Amanda's pulse raced. Even Donelli looked as excited as he ever allowed himself to look before he had a case all tidied up and a suspect jailed.

"Mrs. Cosgrove, you're an angel," he said, kissing her on a papery cheek.

"Young man!" she said indignantly, but the expression in her eyes was suddenly dreamy with memories.

"Come on, Amanda." Donelli grabbed her hand and dragged her toward the door.

"Where are we going?" she asked mechanically, all too conscious of the fact that Donelli was actually touching her and that, angry as she'd been with him recently, she still liked the warm feelings he stirred inside her. Her heart thumped more quickly in agreement.

"To see Mrs. Taylor," he announced.

Amanda grimaced. "Deborah will be ecstatic, I'm sure."

"Don't let the old battle-ax intimidate you. She's really a pushover."

"Maybe for you," she said, then amended, "at least before Henry Taylor got to her. She never did trust me any farther than she could throw me and she could probably heft me clear down the driveway and into that murky goldfish pond."

Donelli gave her shoulders a comforting squeeze. "I'll protect you, Amanda," he vowed solemnly.

"Thanks," she muttered dryly.

Mrs. Cosgrove chuckled at their bickering. "I wouldn't quibble, if I were you, young lady. It's been a long time since I had a hunk like this on my side. If I were a few years younger, I'd snap him right up for myself."

Just what she needed, Amanda thought. Another matchmaker. "Let's get out of here, Donelli."

In the car, he grinned at her. "What's wrong?" he inquired with more amusement than compassion.

"Nothing's wrong," she said, turning the key in the ignition for a second time. The already humming engine squealed in protest. She bit her bottom lip to keep from screaming. Forcing herself not to look at Donelli, she carefully shifted into gear and pulled into the road.

"Why would you think anything was wrong?" she said when she could get the words out without choking on the lie.

"I thought maybe she gave you something to think about."

"She did. Mrs. Taylor's control over that bank."

He laughed. "Nice try, Amanda, but we both know that's not what got you all riled up as we were leaving."

"Donelli, have I ever mentioned that you have an ego the size of Kansas?"

"Be thankful I do. Otherwise, a man could get crushed by your lack of commitment."

"Commitment?" she repeated incredulously, slamming on the brakes and staring at him. He was wearing a pleased expression. She found it particularly obnoxious.

"Where did that remark come from?" she snapped. "If it weren't for this case, we wouldn't even be speaking. A situation, might I remind you, that was your doing."

"I have been trying my damnedest to be fair to you."

"Thank you very much, but I can make my own decisions about which men . . ."

"Men?"

"Man . . . which *man* I want in my life."

-143-

Donelli appeared excessively intrigued by the statement. "Can you really? Does that mean you've finally made a decision about Mack?"

"Yes. No." She braked the car again with a screech of tires. Fortunately they were in front of Mrs. Taylor's house. She turned off the engine and slapped her hand repeatedly against the steering wheel in frustration.

"I guess you need some more time to think things over," Donelli observed. He seemed to be just brimming over with fairness and generosity. Amanda wanted to punch him.

"Just get out of the car, Donelli."

"Whatever you say, Amanda."

Amanda slammed the car door shut and stalked around it in such a fury that she didn't notice that Donelli had stopped in the middle of the walk. She ran smack into him.

He put an arm around her to steady her, which she might have found seductive if she hadn't noticed that he wasn't paying the least bit of attention to her. He was staring at the wide veranda. Amanda looked in the same direction.

"Is that it?" he said, nodding toward the Confederate flag that fluttered in the October breeze.

"I'm no expert, but it sure looks like it to me."

"Well, well. I wonder how it got there."

"We're not going to find out standing out here."

They found Mrs. Taylor waiting for them in the parlor. Deborah escorted them in. Amanda was sure she caught a triumphant, I-told-you-so gleam in the housekeeper's beady little eyes, but she didn't give her the satisfaction of asking her about that flag.

She wasn't nearly as reticent with Mrs. Taylor. As soon as she'd introduced Donelli, she blurted, "When did you get your flag back?"

"My flag? What on earth do you mean? As far as I know, it's still missing."

"Not anymore. Come, take a look."

Mrs. Taylor popped to her feet and hurried through the house, her motions as spry as Amanda had ever seen them. She flipped on the porch light and stared at the flagpole that extended above the eaves. She looked as if she'd seen a ghost.

"Oh, my," she whispered, her fingers fluttering nervously to cover her mouth. Her anxious gaze darted to Amanda. "It's not that I'm not glad it's back, but how do you suppose it got there?"

"The same way it left, I suspect. It wasn't here when we stopped by earlier. Has anyone been by to visit?"

"Not a soul since I got back from town."

"Thomas wasn't here today?" Amanda persisted.

"No. His arthritis was acting up pretty bad. I told him to stay home. His helper wasn't here today either. I suppose anyone could have snuck up on the porch and put it back. I wouldn't have heard them from the back room."

"Mrs. Taylor, you're shivering," Amanda said, noting that she was also far too pale. "Let's go back inside and think about this. I'm sure we can come up with a logical explanation.''

When they were seated in the parlor, Mrs. Taylor asked in a wavery voice, ''Would you like tea, children?''

''Nothing, thank you, Mrs. Taylor,'' Amanda said, catching sight of the tears welling up in the widow's eyes. ''Are you feeling okay? Perhaps I should call your doctor or Henry Junior.''

''That won't be necessary. I'm just fine . . . or at least I was,'' she said. ''But this . . .'' She waved a hand toward the front of the house. ''I just don't understand. You're going to think I'm nothing but a loony old lady after this.''

''We do not think you're one bit loony, Mrs. Taylor,'' Donelli said, hunkering down beside her and taking her hand in his. Tears clogged Amanda's throat at his gentle, reassuring tone. This was the Donelli who'd crept into her heart when she'd least expected it, when she'd been resisting everyone and everything in Georgia. She'd had a chip on her shoulder the size of Manhattan and he'd deftly knocked it off with unexpected glimpses of his tenderness and sensitivity.

''It's clear to us that someone's playing tricks on you,'' he said. ''Do you have any idea who that might be?''

Mrs. Taylor shook her head, still looking miserable. ''I can't think of a soul.''

Amanda and Donelli exchanged a glance.

''Let's talk about something else for a minute, then,'' Donelli suggested. ''We were wondering earlier about your role at the bank. Mrs. Cosgrove mentioned that you have a seat on the board."

She sniffed, drew out a lace-edged hanky scented with lilac, and dabbed at her tears. "Indeed, I do," she said with more vigor. "I was as stunned as anybody at the reading of the will, but the attorneys said Henry had insisted."

"Do you ever exercise your voting privilege?"

"I usually leave that to Henry Junior. He knows much more about these matters than I do. I know that's not what Henry Senior intended, but I can't help it. I just don't care about that sort of thing."

"So Henry Junior would have nothing to gain by trying to get the seat away from you?"

"Heavens no. Everything will be his one day, anyway. This house. Whatever money there is. I always felt bad that his father tied up his inheritance. It's always been my intention that he have it back when I'm gone."

"What if he doesn't want to wait?" Amanda murmured. Mrs. Taylor heard her.

"Young lady, if you are implying that Henry is trying to make me out to be incompetent for some reason, you couldn't be more wrong. We've always had a wonderful relationship. That boy is like a real son to me. I married his father when Henry Junior was little more than a toddler."

"But what if he were in financial difficulty?"

"Why, I'm quite sure he would simply come to me. He

and his father didn't always get on so well. Frankly, I thought Henry Senior was far too hard on him, but I've never denied him anything.''

"I'm sure you haven't," Donelli soothed, unconsciously slipping back into their unplanned good cop–bad cop pattern.

"Mrs. Taylor," Amanda began, intending to ask a few more hard questions about Henry Junior's business practices, financial status, and reaction to being essentially cut out of his daddy's will.

"That's enough for now, Amanda," Donelli said.

"But . . ."

"Enough."

Deborah appeared in the doorway, ending the argument. "Ms. Roberts, you have a call," she announced grudgingly.

Amanda nodded as Donelli continued to pat Mrs. Taylor's frail hand. He stared pointedly at Amanda, then turned to the housekeeper.

"Deborah, I think Mrs. Taylor could probably use a cup of tea," he said. Deborah regarded him suspiciously. Finally, with an indignant huff, she left, presumably to get the tea, though Amanda wouldn't have put it past her to go into the kitchen and sulk.

Amanda followed her in search of the phone. She wanted to use whichever one Deborah had taken the call on, if at all possible. She didn't want to risk the housekeeper lingering on the extension. In the kitchen Deborah gestured toward the receiver sitting atop a pile of well-used cook-books.

"This is Amanda Roberts," she told the caller.

"Miz Roberts, I don't know if you remember, but you told me I should call if anything happened," a vaguely familiar male voice said in a rush.

"Clement?"

"Yes."

"How did you find me?"

"I called your office. They said you'd gone to see Miz Cosgrove. She told me you were at Miz Taylor's."

"Has something happened?"

"I'm not really sure."

"What does that mean?"

"Today's my day at Miz Henderson's. Remember I told you I worked at her place one day a week, just like I do at Miz Taylor's and Miz Cosgrove's?"

Amanda had to try very hard not to scream at him to get to the point. "Is that where you are now?"

"No, I'm down at the gas station now, at a pay phone. That's why I'm calling. I got there today and no one answered the door. Miz Henderson's pretty old and all, but she usually doesn't forget when I'm coming. If she'd gone away or something, she would have left a message with my grandmother or told one of the other ladies. I was thinking maybe she was in there sick or something, but then I got to thinking about all that weird stuff you were telling me about and I decided I'd better call you."

"You haven't called the police?"

"I didn't know if I should."

"Call them, Clement. I'll be right there. I'm only a couple of blocks away. And Clement, whatever you do, don't go in that house. Wait for me outside."

"You don't think she's . . ." Suddenly he sounded scared. Amanda couldn't blame him. She wasn't so wild about the possibilities herself.

CHAPTER

Ten

Getting out of the house in a hurry without further alarming Mrs. Taylor was going to be a neat trick. Amanda was tempted to slip out the backdoor, but she wanted Donelli with her and he was still in the parlor with the already anxious widow. Torn between manners and the need for speed, Amanda chose expediency. She apologized to Mrs. Taylor, leaned down, and whispered an abbreviated version of the emergency into Donelli's ear.

Donelli nodded and stood up, managing to appear perfectly calm and unhurried. "Mrs. Taylor, we really appreciate all your help. Please call us if you think of anything we should know."

Her nervous gaze darted between them. "Is something wrong? Must you leave right away?"

"It's just a lead we need to check out, nothing for you to worry about," Amanda reassured her.

Mrs. Taylor suddenly drew herself up. "Young lady, I've been around a long time. Don't try fooling me. Something has happened. Now tell me what it is."

Amanda sighed. She knew from past experience that Ellie Mae could be every bit as stubborn and willful as Miss Martha. They might as well answer her now or she'd keep them dawdling here until doomsday. "We don't actually know that anything is wrong," she admitted. "That was Clement Washington on the phone. He's concerned because Mrs. Henderson isn't answering her door."

Mrs. Taylor's eyes widened in alarm. "Louisa? Oh, dear heaven. We must hurry then. She hasn't been well for some time."

"Don't you think you should wait here?" Donelli urged, obviously not yet aware that he was banging his head against a brick wall. "You've had an emotional day yourself."

Mrs. Taylor chided, "This is no time to be thinking of myself, young man. I'm coming with you and that's that. Now let's go."

Without waiting for their response, she bustled briskly through the kitchen, past the startled Deborah who'd apparently been lurking outside the parlor door. Grabbing up a collection of keys from a hook near the door, Mrs. Taylor led them outside, then plunged straight ahead into the shadowy walkways of her formal boxwood garden.

Amanda glanced at Donelli, who shrugged in resignation. They hurried after her. Once they'd started through the maze, Amanda was delighted that Mrs. Taylor was leading the way. She lost her sense of direction almost immediately. Whoever had designed the garden had not been fully aware of the mathematical truth that the shortest distance between two points is a straight line. Or maybe he just hadn't been concerned about the need to get to the next street in a hurry.

"Who the devil is this Clement Washington?" Donelli demanded as they finally emerged from the winding route through the boxwoods. They squeezed between the forsythia bushes on the neighboring property and rushed down the street toward Mrs. Henderson's. Motivated by concern for her friend, Mrs. Taylor moved awfully quickly for a woman her age.

"He's a handyman who works for all of the ladies who've been having problems," Amanda explained.

Donelli's hand wrapped around her elbow and jerked her to a stop. "There is a common link among all of these women and you haven't mentioned it before? Where's your head, Amanda?"

Her chin rose. "I interviewed him. He can't be the thief. You'll see when you meet him. He's devoted to Miss Martha, for one thing."

Donelli groaned. "Most con men appear to be devoted to their marks. That's how they get to them," he reminded her, his expression displaying a too-familiar scorn.

"He didn't do it," Amanda insisted.

"What makes you so sure? Your feminine intuition again? Did he flex his muscles and wink at you a couple of times?"

She yanked her arm out of his grip. "Joe Donelli, that is the most sexist remark you have ever made to me. I do not succumb to biceps and winks, as you should perfectly well know. If that were the case, I would have chosen you over Mack long ago and we'd be past this ridiculous bickering."

"Children," Mrs. Taylor said gently, stepping between them. "Don't you think you should put aside your argument for the moment, so we can check on Louisa?" She pointed toward the front door of the smallest of the houses being featured in Amanda's upcoming story. Clement Washington was pacing up and down the porch, puffing on a cigarette. At least this time it was of the legal variety, Amanda noted as he joined them.

"What took you so long?" he asked.

"Don't ask," Amanda replied. "Have you knocked on the door again?"

"No need to waste time with that," Mrs. Taylor said. "I have a key. She gave it to me for times like this. I'll just go right in."

"You will not!" Amanda and Donelli said together.

"I'll go in," Donelli said, taking the key.

"You want me to come along?" Clement offered, appearing braver now that he was in the company of a man who seemed to know what he was doing.

"Probably a good idea. At least she knows you. She might get upset if a strange man comes bounding through the door."

"Which is exactly why I should be the one to go in," Mrs. Taylor said.

Amanda put her hand on the older woman's shoulder. "I think we'd better wait," she said gently.

"But don't you think I should call out to her at least?"

"No, let's leave it to the men, just in case there's a problem."

Mrs. Taylor peered at her anxiously. "You think there's someone else in there or that she's . . . You think she's dead, don't you?"

Donelli and Clement used Mrs. Taylor's distraction as the perfect opportunity to slip through the door. Amanda reminded herself to get even with Donelli later for leaving her to face the really rotten questions all alone.

"I really don't know what to think," Amanda swore.

"She's probably just had one of her spells," Mrs. Taylor said, apparently as much to reassure herself as Amanda. She had taken her handkerchief from her pocket and was twisting it into knots. "She's prone to fainting spells, you know. Always has been. Even when we were girls, Louisa would pass right out in the middle of the sidewalk sometimes. I've told her and told her she shouldn't be living alone, but she won't hear of moving into one of those nursing homes. Can't say as I blame her. I wouldn't want to give up my independence. Still and all, the idea of her being in here all alone and sick is just awful. Maybe I should insist she move in with me. That would be one answer, I suppose. What do you think?''

Mrs. Taylor had rattled on so fast, Amanda could barely keep track of the conversation. Before she could respond, she heard Donelli's footsteps on the stairs. He was making far more noise returning than he had going in. Either he'd found Mrs. Henderson and she was too ill to care about the clattering—or worse. For some reason, it didn't even occur to her to consider the possibility that she'd just gone out for a walk or something. An ominous feeling had settled over her the minute she'd received the call from Clement.

She studied Donelli's somber expression and instinctively reached for Mrs. Taylor's hand. "Is she . . ."

He touched her cheek, then squeezed Mrs. Taylor's shoulder. "Everything's okay. She's in her room. I think she'd very much like to see you, Mrs. Taylor."

To her credit Ellie Mae didn't waste time asking a lot of silly questions. She merely nodded and hurried off up the stairs. Amanda took one step to follow, but Donelli held her back.

"Give them some time alone."

"They're not alone. Clement is up there."

"Just until Mrs. Taylor gets upstairs."

"Is Mrs. Henderson ill?"

"Not physically. She's just terrified."

"Terrified? Of what? Has she been threatened? Did someone break in?"

"I don't think so, but all these thefts apparently have spooked her. She's convinced someone is going to break in here and shoot her to get the family heirlooms. She was sitting up there in a rocking chair with a shotgun across her knees. If Clement hadn't been along, she probably would have blown my head right off. You could be right about him, by the way."

"Thank you very much."

Donelli ignored the intended sarcasm and added, "I've never seen a kid his age handle an old lady so gently."

"It's probably because of his grandmother. I'm not sure if she raised him or not, but he talks about her all the time. She was a big influence in his life."

Just then Clement came back down the stairs and at the same time a very angry Sheriff Eldon Mason appeared in the doorway. He took off his hat, rubbed his hand through sandy red hair, and scowled at the trio of intruders. He did it all in slow motion, either because that was his normal speed of movement or to allow their trepidation at being caught in the act to build.

"Boy," he said, directing his remarks to Clement. "I thought I told you to stick around outside. I ought to take every last one of you in for breaking and entering."

"Settle down, Eldon. Nobody broke in here," Donelli

said. "Mrs. Taylor had a key. She's upstairs with Mrs. Henderson now."

Eldon looked disappointed, but he finally rallied at the news. "Everything okay up there?"

"She wasn't feeling well, that's all."

"Want me to call and get her doc over here?"

"I'm sure Mrs. Taylor will take care of that, if she thinks it's necessary."

"I suppose maybe I ought to just stick my head in up there to be sure they don't need nothing."

"They don't need to be disturbed," Donelli said. "I'm telling you that everything is under control."

Donelli's dismissal clearly irritated the sheriff, but he didn't seem to know quite what to do about it. He rubbed his head again, as if trying to spur his brain into quicker action. Finally, apparently unable to think of any legitimate reason to linger, he said, "You all just call down to the station, if you need anything else."

"We will," Amanda assured him.

When Sheriff Mason had left, Clement said to Amanda, "I think Miz Henderson wants to see you. She wants to know what you're doing to catch the thieves."

Donelli shook his head. "By all means, Amanda, go tell her what *you're* doing."

"Why don't we all go," she suggested diplomatically. "What she really wants is reassurance that she's not the next target and I don't think any of us can give her that."

Clement's expression turned thoughtful. "Maybe I

should offer to stay here for the next few days," he said to Amanda. "What do you think? I could bring a sleeping bag and hang out on the porch. I wouldn't mind."

"It might be a good idea," she agreed. "What do you think, Joe?"

Donelli appeared to be giving the idea careful consideration. "It might be good to have someone around, just to put her mind at ease. There's something you'd have to understand, though. At the first sign of trouble, you call the sheriff. You don't try to handle it on your own and you stay away from that shotgun she has upstairs."

"No problem," Clement vowed, grinning at Amanda as if they shared a huge joke. She caught herself smiling back.

"What was that all about?" Donelli asked as they went upstairs.

"Clement has no use for guns. We had a long talk on the subject, when I was trying to discover if he had been the one to steal Miss Martha's. He won't go near the things."

"A boy after your own heart," Donelli commented with a distinct emphasis on *boy*. Amanda assumed he was trying to send her a message about the pitfalls of May-September romances. She smiled serenely, as if she had a secret of her own. Donelli was frowning by the time they got to Mrs. Henderson's room.

They did their best to reassure the frail old woman that she wasn't in any danger. She was delighted at the prospect of having Clement around for a few days and promised to get on the phone right away and clear it with his other employers. Amanda could see her color and spirits picking up as they talked.

"Why don't we all go downstairs and have a nice cup of tea?" Mrs. Henderson suggested, reaching for her robe. "It won't take me a minute."

"There's no need for you to go rushing around," Amanda said. "Donelli and I really should be going. We're just glad you're okay."

"I am, thanks to this young man." She clung to Clement's hand. "Such a responsible boy, don't you agree? I do wish there were enough for him to do around here full time, but I know once he goes off to college, he won't want to be doing yard work anymore."

"I'll be over here anytime you need me," he promised. "Now I'm just gonna go get my sleeping bag and I'll be back. Once I'm here, you won't have a thing to worry about, Miz Henderson. Nobody'll bother you with me around."

As Clement was leaving, the phone rang. Mrs. Henderson answered the call on her bedside phone, then handed it to Donelli.

Amanda watched his face as he listened. His mumbled, one-word responses gave her no clue at all about what was being said on the other end. His expression, however, was a dead giveaway. It was totally blank. He only kept that straight-faced look when he didn't want to set off alarms.

"What is it now?" she demanded the instant he'd hung up.

"Nothing," he said, even as he began propelling her toward the door.

"Donelli, don't you . . ."

"Amanda," he warned in a low voice. "Later."

When they were safely outside the house and on their way back to her car at Mrs. Taylor's, she said, "Okay, what's going on? Why didn't you want to talk back there?"

"Because there was no need to upset those two ladies any more than they already are."

"Upset them? Will you just spill it? What's happened?"

"That was Mr. Davenport on the phone. Apparently our meeting the other day put the fear of God into him. He has a prospective client right now that he thought we ought to know about. He was livid because he's spent the last hour trying to track us down. Apparently Deborah wasn't interested in seeing that he reached us."

"Who's the client? Is it the same person who brought in the gun? Was she back to check on it?"

"No, this woman has a Confederate flag she wants to auction. She's claiming to be Mrs. Eleanor Mae Taylor."

Amanda stared at him incredulously. "What?"

"You heard me."

"But the flag is back and we both know that Mrs. Taylor is nowhere near Atlanta."

"I know. It gets curiouser and curiouser, doesn't it?"

When they were in the car, Donelli said idly, "I'd step

on it, if I were you, Amanda. I'm not sure how long our Mr. Davenport can hang on to our suspect.''

She shot an astonished gaze in his direction, but she didn't need additional encouragement. The trip across I-20 was made in record time, even by her standards. She squeezed the car into a no-parking zone in front of Willoughby's. Donelli was out of the car before she could even remove the keys from the ignition.

It was just after nine o'clock. The lights in the main showroom were out, but there was a glow toward the back, apparently from the office area. Donelli tried the door. It was locked. He pounded against the glass and finally Mr. Davenport scurried down the corridor. He unlocked the door and stepped back, his expression even more harried than it had been the last time they'd seen him.

"I couldn't keep her here," he said in a rush. "I really tried. I used every excuse I could think of. I told her I was trying to reach a prospective buyer and that if she'd wait just a few more minutes, we could probably conclude the sale tonight.''

Amanda's spirits sank. "She didn't believe you?"

Mr. Davenport shook his head. "I should have realized she would know that isn't our usual procedure. She obviously realized something was wrong. She took off right away.''

"Did she leave the flag?"

Looking absolutely miserable, he shook his head. "No.

She said she'd bring it back if she decided to go through with the sale. She said the flag had a lot of sentimental value and she'd just wanted to explore the possibility of selling it. I doubt we'll see her again. You learn to tell these things. If someone leaves without committing, they probably won't be back."

Amanda sank down in a chair and sighed. Donelli stood behind her and put his hands on her shoulders. He began slowly kneading the knotted muscles as he tried to get a description of the woman from Mr. Davenport. But for all of his attention to detail when it came to antiques, the dealer was lousy as an eyewitness.

"But you're sure it wasn't the same woman who was here before?" Donelli asked again and again.

"Absolutely not," he repeated. "I'm sure her hair color was different and they weren't the same size. They didn't make the same overall impression at all. This woman was classier, if you know what I mean. That's why I should have been more cautious. She's probably dealt with us before. She obviously knew the procedure."

"Don't beat yourself up over this," Donelli said. "You tried."

"The pictures," Amanda said, suddenly seizing on the one avenue of identification they hadn't tried.

"What pictures?" Donelli said. His hands paused in their seductive massage. Mr. Davenport stared.

"The ones from Miss Martha's party. Maybe he'll be

able to identify the women from those. They could have been there." She turned to Mr. Davenport who was looking more hopeful. "Do you think you'd recognize them?"

"I'm sure of it. I may not be good with details, but I do remember a specific look, a style."

"It's worth a shot, then. I'll bring the pictures by in the morning," Amanda promised. "What time do you get in?"

"Generally not until ten, but I'd be happy to come in earlier, if it would help."

"No," Amanda said, thinking of the long drive home she had yet tonight and the drive back in the morning. "Ten will be fine."

Donelli's hands tightened briefly on her shoulders. "Let's go, Amanda. It's been a long day."

Outside, in the glow of the street lamp, he held out his hand for the keys. She met his gaze and saw the determination, along with something else—a familiar look that made her heart race. Her breath caught and she hesitated, terrified that she was misreading his intentions.

"Your car's here in town," she reminded him.

His unblinking gaze never left her face. "I know. I'll get it in the morning."

"Joe, are you sure?"

A faint, rueful smile crossed his face. "I've never been the one who was unsure, Amanda. I love you."

She nodded. She recognized the unwavering truth of the

statement, a truth she had all too often taken for granted while not examining her own emotions at all. "I'm still mixed up," she admitted with more candor than usual. "With everything that's gone on the last few weeks, it's been the wrong time to try to make a decision like this. I haven't even spent any time with Mack to see if there's anything left."

"I know that, too. I told you I'd wait as long as it took. Tonight, though, I want you back in my arms. I want to remind you of what we have together." He paused while her heart hammered unsteadily. "If that's what you want."

She drew in a deep, steadying breath and placed the keys in his hand. "Let's go home."

CHAPTER
Eleven

There was an edge of desperation to Donelli's love-making that carried Amanda over the edge and back again and again. Cupping her face in his callused palms, he kissed her, feather-light kisses, followed by deep, hungry claimings that sent a wicked heat flowing through her. His touches caressed gently, then demanded, setting her skin on fire and leaving her senses shattered. With each long, slow stroke—along the curve of her hip, up the sensitive flesh of her thigh—he told her how he felt, filling her head with promises and her heart with love. Even without words, in his arms she found again the sense of peace and satisfaction that had been missing for these last lonely weeks. Her body throbbed with an intimate awareness of the man whose arm curved possessively around her waist, whose breath whispered against her breast.

And the slow, fevered rise of passion began again.

"This is what we can have, Amanda," he told her, poised above her, holding her at the edge of the brink, taunting her with possibilities.

His eyes darkening with desire, he repeated, "This, Amanda."

And each slow, deep thrust fulfilled the sensual promise.

But for all the fiery passion, all the mind-numbing explosions of feeling, it was the tenderness that drew her in, the forever commitment she could see in his eyes. So many questions remained, but one had been answered beyond all doubt: Joe's love for her was unselfish and enduring. Even in sending her back to Mack, he had been demonstrating the depth of his love. Now, with the patience that often drove her crazy, he waited for her decision, waited for her to discover what was in her heart.

And fitting her body to his, taking his silken heat deep inside her, she tried to show him what was there. For now. For this moment. And maybe for all time.

Exhausted, her body slick with sweat, Amanda rested in Joe's arms. When the tears came unexpectedly to clog her throat and fill her eyes, she prayed he wouldn't notice, but of course he did. His embrace tightened.

"What's wrong?"

"Nothing." A sniff turned the denial into a lie.

"Amanda. Tell me."

A sigh whispered through her. "I want it to be over. I want things to be right between us again."

"I'd say tonight everything was right."

"But you deserve more. You deserve a commitment and I'm terrified to make it. When I'm with you, everything seems so clear, but Mack is always there, always in the shadows. It's like living with a ghost and I don't know how to let it go or even if I want to."

"You'll know when the time is right."

There was that blasted patience again and something else, a note of serene confidence. She levered herself up and peered closely into his eyes. "Do you know something I don't know?"

He chuckled at her indignation. "You really do hate secrets, don't you? It's probably why you became a reporter. Did you peek at your Christmas presents?"

"Don't try to change the subject."

"All I know, Amanda, is what I feel in my heart and what I think you feel in yours. For now, that's enough."

"I want to know too. I hate what I've been doing to you, to us."

"It was my choice, remember. I can live with it." He pressed her head down until it rested against his chest. "Now get some sleep."

But long after Donelli's breathing had settled into a steady rhythm, long after dawn crept over the horizon, she lay wide awake and wondering what would become of them.

* * *

"Stop worrying about us," Donelli told her, tilting her face up for a last, lingering kiss when she dropped him at his car in the morning. "Concentrate on what you need to do today. I don't want you getting careless. Nothing violent has happened so far, but this pattern is beginning to worry me. Somebody is being very methodical. Until we figure out what they're really after, I don't want you taking any risks."

"I'm just going to see Mr. Davenport this morning. Depending on where that leads, I may just try to go home early today. Maybe if I relax for a while, some of the pieces will begin to fall into place."

"I'll call you later. If you're not around, I'll leave a message with Jenny Lee. Check with her if you need to reach me."

For several minutes after he walked away, she sat staring after him. Finally she shook off her dreamy state and went by the office to pick up Larry's contact sheets. At ten o'clock she was in Mr. Davenport's office with the pages spread across his desk. By ten-fifteen, she was pacing. Mr. Davenport was every bit as thorough and patient as Donelli. He used her magnifying loupe to study each tiny print, shaking his head, murmuring under his breath.

"Ah," he exclaimed at one point. Amanda's pulse raced.

"What?" she said, rushing to his side.

"I was just noticing Miss Martha's pin. I recall it being auctioned here."

Deflated, she sat down, tapping her foot impatiently.

"Hmmm," he said thoughtfully. Amanda decided that was even less significant than *ah*. She didn't bother to get up until he gestured for her. "Here, look at this."

"You found her?"

"I believe so. Yes," he said, nodding emphatically. "That's definitely the woman who was here last night. Do you recognize her?"

Amanda bent over the print. The woman he'd indicated was tall, thin, and definitely classy. Her silk dress hung perfectly on what appeared to be a size-eight body. Her dark hair fell in a classic smooth wave to just below her chin. Her features were strong, the mouth a little too wide, the nose a little too long, but the effect was still striking and subtly sensual.

"Well," Mr. Davenport prodded. "Do you know her?"

"She looks familiar, but that could be just because she was at the party. Did you recognize the other woman at all?"

"No. There is no one even remotely like her in these pictures."

"But she had to have been at this party," Amanda said, thinking aloud. "That's the only time she could have taken the gun."

"Perhaps she didn't take it. Perhaps someone else did

and slipped it into a pocket or a purse. It's not a large gun. That would be easy enough to do. Whoever took it probably didn't even leave right away. They probably hung around to see what would happen.''

Amanda stared at him. ''I'm impressed, Mr. Davenport. You could be right.''

''I'm a fan of Sherlock Holmes. I've always wondered what it would be like to be a detective. I hope I've helped somewhat.''

''You have.''

''What will you do now?''

''Take the pictures over to Miss Martha's and get an ID on the woman. I'm sure she knew every one of her guests personally.''

Mr. Davenport cleared his throat. ''Would you mind . . . I mean, if it wouldn't be an intrusion, could I come along?'' A slow flush crept up his neck.

Amanda caught herself before she chuckled aloud. Unless she was imagining things, Mr. William Davenport had developed a fondness for Miss Martha. Now that, she thought with a sort of wicked glee, would be a fascinating match to observe. A first impression would have suggested that Miss Martha would make mincement of a man like Mr. Davenport, but perhaps not. He seemed to have a sharp wit she hadn't credited him with before this morning.

''Come along,'' she said. ''If you don't mind taking your own car. I'm not going to be coming back into Atlanta when I leave there.''

Mr. Davenport beamed. "That's no problem at all. I will meet you there."

To Amanda's further astonishment, he actually beat her there. He was waiting in the driveway when she turned in, an expectant gleam in his eyes.

Della let them in, but Miss Martha was already halfway down the center hallway by the time the door was shut. "Amanda, dear, how are you? And William, what a lovely surprise. Tea? Coffee cake? Della made a cinnamon and nut cake fresh this morning."

"How delightful," Mr. Davenport murmured.

"I'll bring it at once," Della said. She glanced at Amanda. "Coffee for you, miss?"

Amanda caught the glimmer of understanding in the housekeeper's eyes. Well, well. The world was full of surprises this morning. "Yes, Della. Coffee would be wonderful."

Miss Martha chuckled. "You should have spoken up long ago, dear. Della obviously couldn't stand watching you suffer through another cup of tea."

"The tea was . . ."

"Mack's favorite," she said with gentle understanding. "Come, tell me why you've come by. Has there been a break in the case?"

"Possibly," Amanda said, explaining about the photos. She removed the contact sheet from her purse and pointed to the woman Mr. Davenport had identified. She watched Miss Martha's expression closely. There was a flicker of dismay in her eyes. Her lips pursed. And her cane tapped nervously.

"Who is it, Miss Martha?"

There was a seemingly endless hesitation before she said in a tone filled with regret, "Jessica Taylor."

"Henry Junior's wife?" Amanda said with a growing sense of distress that nearly matched Miss Martha's. "Do you suppose he knew what she did to his stepmother?"

"How could he not have known?" Miss Martha said angrily. "He's her husband. I just don't understand it, though. He's always seemed so devoted. Ellie Mae is going to be devastated." Suddenly she paused. "What about the gun, William? Did she have the gun?"

"She was not the woman who brought it to Willoughby's."

"Surely there can't be two thieves on the loose."

"Maybe not," Mr. Davenport reassured her. "Maybe it all fits together somehow. We just have to figure out how."

"In the meantime, what should we do about Ellie Mae?" Miss Martha asked.

"Nothing yet," Amanda said finally. "Let's wait until we get a little more information."

"What about the police?"

"We've never told the police any of this. There's no reason to start now, unless you want to report what happened with the gun."

"No, I still feel as I did before that this is a private matter. We'll handle it as quietly as possible."

"We may have to tell them eventually," Amanda warned. "It may be beyond our control."

"Well, we'll just have to face that when the time comes, won't we?" Miss Martha said staunchly. She turned to Mr. Davenport. "More tea, William?"

"Delightful."

Amanda left them reminiscing about the old days before Atlanta's sprawl enveloped the glorious countryside.

It seemed like a very long trip home. Amanda couldn't shake off the awful discovery about Jessica Taylor's involvement in the theft of Ellie Mae's flag. By the time she pulled into her yard, she was exhausted. She was not in the mood to discover Mack sitting on the porch and a sheriff's car blocking the driveway with the sheriff lounging against the front fender. It did not bode well for the rest of the day.

"What are you doing here?" she asked as she approached the porch. She made the question general, since she wasn't feeling particular about who answered first. She reached instinctively for a handful of jelly beans.

"Waiting for you," the sheriff and Mack chorused.

"Why?" she persisted, hoping for specifics.

"I was planning to ask you to go out for dinner," Mack said.

"I have a warrant to search the house," said Sheriff Eldon Mason.

Amanda wasn't sure which response made her more nervous. The legal implications of the sheriff's announcement, however, seemed to demand an immediate reaction.

"I don't understand," she said to Eldon. "Why on earth would you want to search my house? What are you looking for?"

"A pocket watch belonging to Mrs. Cosgrove over in Madison, for one thing. That's what's mentioned in the warrant, but word has it that I should be on the lookout for any other Civil War memorabilia."

"Are you out of your mind?" Mack and Amanda snapped in unison.

She looked at her ex-husband. "Thank you."

"No problem." He turned to the sheriff. "There must be some mistake. Amanda doesn't go around stealing things."

"It's nice that you trust her, but I can't go and take that as proof now, can I? Not when there have been all these thefts lately and she's the one common link among them."

"Link?" Amanda said incredulously.

"The way I hear it, you been in every one of those houses in the last couple of months."

"Of course I have. I've been working on a feature story. Call my boss."

"No need to do that. He'll just confirm that you've been assigned to do the story. He's got no way of knowing what you did whilst you were visiting. After you've gone, something turned up missing in every one of those places. Sounds mighty suspicious to me. If we find that watch inside, then I'd say it pretty much makes our case."

"This is ridiculous," Amanda repeated. "Other people have been in all of those houses. My photographer for one." She hoped Larry would forgive her for throwing him to the wolves. She was merely trying to make a point. "And the handyman, Clement. You know him. He works at all of those places."

"But nobody swore out a warrant against the two of them," Eldon reminded her.

"I don't believe this."

"Just let the man go conduct his search, Amanda," Mack said, putting an arm around her. "Once he's done, he can apologize and you can sue him for harassment, if you want to."

She glared at the two of them, then finally gave a sigh of resignation. "Go. Search."

She sat down in the rocking chair on the porch and began rocking agitatedly.

"Would you like some iced tea, Amanda?"

"I'd like that man to get out of my house."

"He's just doing his job."

"Since when did you become such a proponent of law and order? Aren't you one of those professors who used to refer to cops as fascist pigs?"

"I've mellowed."

Amanda allowed him to get away with the statement, but only because she wasn't much in the mood to discuss his level of maturity, either past or present.

"Do you want the tea, Amanda?"

"No." She bit her lip, then added more politely, "Thank you."

Mack shrugged. "Whatever. I just want to help."

She was about to tell him what he could do with his help when Eldon emerged. From his triumphant expression, she was pretty sure he'd found more than her lace underwear. A cold shiver of dread darted up her spine.

"I'm afraid I'm going to have to ask you to come with me, miss," he said. He didn't sound one bit sorry about it.

"Why?" Amanda said, not minding at all that he was likely to think her deliberately obtuse.

He reached into his pocket and extracted the pocket watch. "Found this in your dresser drawer. I'd say it just about clinches things."

Amanda glanced at the watch, hoping it would turn out to be some cheap imitation. They made fake Rolexes and fake Guccis. Why not fake antique pocket watches? This one, however, wasn't a fake. She recognized at once that it was the real thing.

She looked at Mack, then turned back to the sheriff. "Can I make a call now or do I have to wait until we get to the station?"

"Now's fine," he said agreeably.

Dazed, she walked inside and dialed Donelli's number.

Fortunately he was at home instead of traipsing all over the countryside.

"I think you'd better meet me at the police station," she said, fighting against the cold fury that was beginning to chase away her panic.

"Why? New information?"

"You might say that. The sheriff thinks he's caught the thief."

"Who is it?"

"Me."

Donelli was still cursing when she hung up.

CHAPTER
Twelve

The one-room jail had once been a White Castle hamburger haven. Amanda was all too familiar with its dreary gray interior and its single cell. Donelli had kept her sitting for hours on one of the uncomfortable straight-backed chairs the night they'd first met. He'd assumed, as Sheriff Mason did now, that torture was conducive to revelations. What neither of them recognized was that she was made of sterner stuff. In this instance, anyway, she also had no revelations to share. She had not stolen Mrs. Cosgrove's antique watch. Worse, from her point of view, she hadn't yet discovered who had ripped it off.

Mack, bless him, was valiantly trying to reach an attorney who'd get down here and get her out before she died of boredom. Not that that was likely to occur tonight.

She was too furious to be bored at the moment. She wanted to identify and then strangle the person who'd set her up.

"The room was made for you," Donelli observed when he finally walked through the door over an hour after she'd called him. She knew exactly how long it took to get from his place to the jail. He'd had time to do that and stop for dinner. It did not incline her to greet him cheerfully. This wasn't the cavalry coming to the rescue. This was the cavalry dropping in to visit.

"What the hell took you so long?" she said.

"I stopped for dinner," he said with an edge of asperity meant to criticize her doubting, irritated tone. He counterpointed his sarcasm by resting a comforting hand on her shoulder and massaging the knots of tension.

"You okay?" he asked in a gentler tone.

She felt the salty sting of tears in her eyes, but she managed to nod. Her temper died as rapidly as it had flared. "Fine. Where have you been really?"

"I've been trying to reach that fool lawyer of Oscar's."

Suddenly panicked, she asked, "You didn't get him, did you?"

"No."

"Thank God!"

"Amanda, what is wrong with you? You need an attorney."

"I know. Mack's trying to reach one now. I don't want Oscar's."

"Why on earth not? This is exactly what the magazine

pays the man that healthy retainer to do. He's supposed to bail you out of jams like this.''

"Think, Donelli. If Randolph Butler comes here, there is no way I'll be able to keep this arrest from Oscar.''

"Why would you want to?''

"Because trumped-up charges or not, he will yank me off this story faster than you can say William Randolph Hearst. Journalists who have been arrested for grand theft are not the most objective individuals to have covering the story.''

"Reporters who have been set up are not especially safe, either. Hasn't it occurred to you that this might be a very good time to take a little vacation? Maybe go visit your family in New York? Fly off and laze around on some beach in the Caribbean? Whatever?''

"I am not running scared, Donelli. It's not my style.''

"More's the pity.''

"You don't really want me to be a coward.''

He sighed. His fingers tangled in her hair and he tilted her face up so he could meet her gaze evenly. "No, but a little display of common sense every now and then wouldn't break me up. Why did you call me, Amanda, if you didn't want my help?''

That was the tough one. She'd known it was coming from the instant she'd dialed the phone, but she'd been no more able to stop herself from placing that call than she had been of leaving her fate in Mack's hands. It wasn't that she trusted Mack any less than she trusted Donelli—

at least not when it came to a situation like this. It was just that Mack didn't know his way around crooks and criminals the way Donelli did.

"I needed your expertise," she said candidly.

She thought the admission was enough, especially for a woman who prided herself on needing no one. But she saw the shadow of hurt in his eyes the instant before a too-bright smile made light of it. "That's me. Always ready to dash to the rescue of a damsel in distress. I assume you have a theory about what happened. Care to share it with me?"

"Not really."

"Then what the hell am I doing here? What expertise were you hoping to tap?"

"You know how to talk to Eldon. I can't seem to get past my inbred biases that men who drawl and wear greasy old baseball caps on the back of their heads don't have brains. It tends to get in the way of rational conversation."

"Meaning that if you don't keep your mouth shut, Eldon might lock you up and throw away the key."

She smiled ruefully. "Afraid so. Will you talk to him?"

"Would it do any good to put a condition on my cooperation?"

"It depends on the condition."

"I refer you back to the vacation opportunities presented earlier."

"Not a chance."

"I could just leave you here."

"You could, but you won't. You know that sooner or later Mack will find an attorney and he'll get me out of here. You don't want to give your competition that sort of an edge, do you?"

The taunt was a mistake. She knew it from the immediate glint of fury in his eyes and the locking of his jaw. Whatever progress they'd made the night before was wiped out by a single, unthinking remark. She'd meant it as no more than a pathetic attempt at humor, a teasing challenge, but to Donelli it was obviously no joke. He turned without saying a word and walked out.

"Donelli," she said plaintively.

He didn't even break stride. He kept right on going.

Helpless to do anything about it, while Eldon had her more or less obligated to remain right where she was, she turned her attention back to Mack, who was still on the phone. "Any luck?" she called across the room.

"I have talked to three answering services, two children under the age of six, and a wife who told me to let her know if I tracked down her rotten spouse in any of the bars around town. Are you sure you won't let me call that fancy lawyer Oscar put on retainer?"

Amanda groaned. "I have already had this conversation twice tonight. Once with you on the way over here and once with Donelli. I do not intend to go through it again. The answer is still no, Mack. Not if I have to rot in here. I will not put myself in a position to be taken off this story."

"You won't be able to pursue your hot story from inside a jail cell."

"Maybe not, but I can dream up some dandy revenge. Just keep trying the others."

Mack shook his head, but apparently he finally decided to yield to her stubbornness. He picked up the receiver and dialed another number from the yellow pages.

While Mack talked to yet another answering service, Donelli came back into the jailhouse, followed by a pensive Eldon. The sheriff turned a chair around backward and straddled it. He removed his baseball cap. It improved her ability to take him seriously.

"You know, Ms. Roberts, it seemed to me earlier that you have a real bad attitude. One of them snippy, big-city attitudes, know what I mean?"

Amanda declined to comment.

"Oftentimes," he went on, "that's the kind of thing that makes me think a person is covering something up. Joe here, he believes you're innocent."

Amanda shot a grateful look at Donelli, but he was pointedly ignoring her. "I am," she swore solemnly. She kept her response to a minimum in an attempt to assure that she wouldn't blow this unexpected mellowing of moods. She had a feeling the rapport was tenuous at best.

"He also says I can trust you to get yourself back down here for more questions the minute I call."

"Absolutely."

"He also says you won't do a thing to interfere with this investigation."

She had to bite her tongue at that one.

"No comment?" he inquired with the first touch of genuine amusement she'd seen in him.

She found herself smiling, albeit faintly. "I think it might be best if I plead the Fifth."

"Wise move," Donelli concurred. "I think the best you can hope for, Eldon, is a promise that she'll share any evidence she turns up. Isn't that right, Amanda?"

She didn't hear any room for argument in his tone. "Right," she promised reluctantly.

"Immediately," Eldon amended with an insulting lack of trust.

"I'll share the evidence," she repeated.

Eldon and Donelli sighed.

"Ms. Roberts, I don't envy the man who has to cope with that stubborn streak of yours."

"Amen," Mack and Donelli agreed in unison.

Amanda glared at both of the traitors. "Let's just get out of here," she snapped, grabbing her purse and stalking out the door.

In the parking lot, she was faced with a choice—Mack's car or Donelli's. With either one of them, she was bound to get an unwanted lecture. If it weren't such a long way home and so late at night, she'd choose to walk.

Donelli made it easy for her. "Go on home and get some rest, Amanda. I'll see you in the morning."

It was too easy. She stared at him distrustfully. "Where are you going?"

"Don't worry about it."

"I am not worried about it. I just want to know."

"Would you believe me if I told you that it has nothing to do with the case?"

"Not if you're trying to convince me that you have a hot date across town. That's not your style, Donelli. Not after last night."

"Are you so sure, Amanda? Maybe seeing you with your ex has driven me into the arms of another woman."

He winked when he said it. Mack regarded them speculatively. What drove Amanda nuts all the way home was her uncertainty over the meaning of that wink. She wrestled with an uncommon bout of jealousy so sharp and painful it left her speechless. In turn, that gave Mack the opportunity to remind her all the way home that she was going to have to be more careful, that she was obviously the target of someone dangerous, that she ought to consider taking a trip, preferably with him.

Except for that last bit about taking off with him, he sounded exactly like Donelli. When they arrived at her house, she got out of the car, thanked him for his advice, and told him to go home. Also like Donelli, he paid no attention to her. He was still lecturing her when she slammed the bedroom door in his face.

He opened it and followed her in. He picked up a nightgown that had been tossed on the floor and held it out to her.

"Go away," she said, taking it from him and stuffing it into the laundry hamper before he could begin to wonder when she'd started wearing such sexy, lacy confections.

"We need to talk."

"Not tonight."

"Then in the morning. I'll stay here. You shouldn't be alone tonight anyway."

At her look of immediate alarm, he smiled sadly. "On the couch, if you prefer."

"You don't need to stay here." What she didn't say was that if Donelli had really feared that there was any danger, he'd be here himself. He wasn't, ergo she was safe and she really wanted to be by herself. She wanted to think about the case. She needed to think about why she'd turned instinctively to Donelli when she was in trouble, even with Mack right beside her.

"I want to stay here," he repeated.

"Mack, that sofa is hard as a rock. It's too short for you. And I don't want you here. Am I getting through to you?"

"I'm conversant in English, Amanda."

"I realize that, but are you listening? I want to be alone." How had she forgotten that Mack was every bit as stubborn as she was? How had she dismissed his tendency to ignore her wishes and blindly set off on his own chosen course? She should have recalled the faculty teas he'd dragged her to over her protests, the number of times he'd given her gifts of books on subjects that fascinated him but meant nothing to her.

"And I don't think you should be by yourself," he repeated with an uncanny lack of understanding of her needs. There was no point arguing with him if he was going to be intentionally obtuse. Since she wasn't about to attempt to throw him out bodily or to call the cops, she shrugged.

"Fine, stay. Why should I care if your back kills you all day tomorrow? Just do me one favor?" she said, pushing him through the bedroom doorway.

His expression brightened. "Anything."

"Don't be here when I get up in the morning."

She shut the door very quietly behind him and turned the lock. It wasn't that she didn't trust her ex. She just wanted to make a point.

She doubted if he'd get it.

CHAPTER
Thirteen

Amanda awoke with a splitting headache to the sound of her shower running. If she was lucky, it was a leak. More likely, it was Mack. Obviously, he hadn't taken the hint. She shouldn't really have been surprised. He never had paid any attention to her when she talked, a fact she'd almost forgotten until yesterday.

Indignation mounting at his audacity in lingering on when she'd pointedly told him to be gone by morning, she stormed into the bathroom. Unmindful of the dictates of modesty or even common sense, she yanked back the shower curtain, reached in, and flipped off the hot water. Mack's howl of outrage over the icy drenching gave her immense satisfaction.

That gloating sensation might have kept her going all

day, but when she walked into the kitchen, she found Donelli methodically removing eggs, milk, butter, and orange juice from the refrigerator. If yesterday had been the worst day of her life, what did that make this? Her first day in Hell?

"I thought you could probably use a good breakfast this morning," Donelli announced cheerfully. "Coffee?"

She was torn between the need to demonstrate her irritation at his presumption and the even greater desire for caffeine-induced salvation. She opted for the caffeine.

"I'm surprised Mack let you in," she muttered, sipping at the dark, rich blend of coffee.

His hand, clutching a whisk, paused above the eggs. "Mack?"

She studied his instantly wary expression. "You didn't know he was here?"

"How the hell would I know he was here? I am not used to finding strange men in your house at the crack of dawn."

"Mack is not a strange man. He's my ex-husband."

"Stranger still. Did you invite him to stay?"

She chuckled. "Hardly. Didn't you hear him scream just now?"

"You're not always at your best in the morning. I figured you'd gotten up on the wrong side of the bed."

"Thanks."

"What exactly was Mack doing in your shower?" he

growled, whipping the eggs so hard Amanda had to turn away to hide a grin. "Doesn't his work?"

"Why don't you ask the question that's really on your mind? You want to know if I slept with him?"

Donelli threw down the whisk, walked over, and planted both hands firmly on the table in front of her. He leaned down until his brown eyes were level with hers. "Yes, Amanda. Yes, I think I do want to know exactly that. Have you taken to sleeping with your ex again?"

She decided she'd taunted him just about as far as she dared. She shook her head. "No. I didn't sleep with him."

Just then, Mack wandered into the kitchen, a towel wrapped around his hips and fury in his eyes.

"Amanda, what the hell did you think you were doing in there just now?" he said before he caught sight of Donelli. His gazed narrowed.

Joe smiled. Apparently her denial of a renewed relationship with Mack had cheered him up. "Morning, Roberts. Enjoy your shower?"

Mack hitched the towel more securely around his waist. "What are you doing here at this hour?"

"I stopped by to fix Amanda some breakfast. Care to join us?"

Mack seemed to ponder the alternatives. With a resigned shrug, he finally said, "Yeah, sure. Why not? I'll be back in a minute."

Left alone, Donelli dropped the friendly demeanor. He

turned his back on Amanda and whipped the eggs more ferociously than before. He went back to the refrigerator and searched for cheese, then set about grating the block of cheddar. When he scraped his knuckles on the grater, he swore indignantly.

Amanda stood up and reached for his hand. "Let me see."

"It's nothing."

"I'm not in the mood for your tough guy routine, Donelli. Let me see it."

She held his bleeding fist under the cold water, then reached for the bottle of peroxide she kept next to the sink and doused his hand liberally. He yelped.

"You enjoyed that," he accused.

She smiled serenely. "Yes, I did."

When Mack returned he regarded the two of them warily, then walked over to the cupboards and took down a stack of plates. He opened the drawer in which she kept the stainless steel flatware and methodically went about setting the table. His actions only served to further irritate Donelli, who went in search of the napkins.

"You're out of napkins," he announced.

"Amanda is always out of napkins," Mack countered with pointed familiarity. "There are cloth ones in that drawer by the refrigerator."

"I know where the damn napkins are," Donelli growled, grabbing three from the drawer and putting them on the table. He picked up the plates Mack had just set out and put them in a neat stack by the stove. "Amanda, where'd you put the omelet pan? I couldn't find it with the other pans."

"Try the drawer under the oven," Mack suggested.

"There are no pans . . ." Donelli began as Mack reached past him, opened the drawer, and retrieved the omelet pan.

"That's where we kept it in New York," Mack said. "Sometimes she forgets."

The whole process of getting breakfast on the table was beginning to wear Amanda out. Given a choice, she'd have gone out for pancakes and left the two of them fussing and feuding over the pans and table settings. Exhaustion and curiosity were the only things that kept her where she was to observe this male territorial ritual. Besides, she wanted to know what Donelli had really been up to when he left her last night. Sometime around dawn she'd finally convinced herself that she'd been crazy to imagine that he really would have run off to another woman. That meant he'd been doing some investigating. Sooner or later he was bound to fill her in on what he'd discovered.

She also knew that she needed both Mack and Joe on her side. In fact, she could use all the friends she could get. Even though Eldon had released her after questioning the night before, the presence of that stolen watch in her house was not likely to be forgotten unless she could come up with a reasonable explanation and enough evidence to support it.

"I know you two are probably enjoying this chance to get to know each other," she said, stepping between them the way a referee occasionally gets between two boxers intent on punching each other out after the bell. "But it would be really helpful if we could all put our heads together and try to figure out how the hell that watch turned up in my dresser drawer."

"Someone obviously planted it," Mack said.

"Thank you, Sherlock Holmes," she muttered. "Any idea who that someone might have been?"

"We have several possible motives at work here," Donelli said. "First, someone took those things hoping to sell them for what they're worth. Second, someone wanted to suggest that one or all of those ladies were getting senile. Third, the whole thing was a plot to set up Amanda."

"Not the whole thing," she corrected. "My name was never connected with any of the attempts to fence things through Mr. Davenport."

"Very good, Amanda," Donelli said approvingly.

She gritted her teeth at the patronizing tone. "Thank you for your support."

He ignored the sarcasm. "That means," he said with an emphasis that suggested the interruption was unappreciated, "the attempt to implicate you was something new, a last-minute change. Why?"

"Obviously, it has something to do with the story," Mack said. "When Amanda turned this into something more than a light little piece of fluff, it apparently made someone nervous. Planting the watch was a way to side-track her.''

''Unless,'' she said, ''they never wanted the story done in the first place and hoped to make all those ladies seem so crazy that Oscar would back off giving them a forum.''

''So, you think this is something more than a personal thing between Mrs. Taylor and her family,'' Donelli said.

''It has to be. Otherwise why involve the other two women?''

''I'm inclined to agree,'' Mack said. ''There's a big picture here that we're just not getting. What's the one thing all those ladies have in common?''

''Money.''

''No. Mrs. Cosgrove is fresh out. That's why she's been selling her land off bit by bit,'' Amanda reminded them. ''I don't think that's common knowledge, but she admitted it to me when I was working on the story.''

''Which is why she does her own dusting,'' Donelli concluded thoughtfully. ''Of course.''

''Congratulations,'' Amanda said. ''I hold out some hope for your career as a private investigator after all.''

''Don't be too quick to congratulate me. I should have picked up on that the other night. Who's she been selling the land to?''

Amanda shrugged. ''I didn't get into that with her.''

''Maybe it's time you did.''

"Fine. I'll call her now."

Mack was shaking his head. "Not a good idea. She may not be convinced that you weren't the one who walked off with her prized possession."

"All the more reason I should go to see her. She needs to hear what happened from me."

Donelli stared hard at Mack. "How long were you two married?"

"Five years. Why?"

"I'm amazed you actually think you can talk Amanda out of doing something, once she's made up her mind."

"The secret is to get to her before her mind is made up. I thought for a minute there that I might have a shot at it."

Amanda stood up and headed for the door while the two men continued to analyze what they considered to be her quixotic behavior. When they realized that she was abandoning them, they had to run to catch up with her.

"Mack, don't you have classes or something?" she asked pointedly.

"I'll call and cancel them."

"Don't. I don't want you disrupting your life for me. I can handle Henrietta Cosgrove."

Donelli was lounging against the side of her car listening to the exchange. He seemed to take great satisfaction in watching her dismissal of Mack.

"You, too, Donelli," she said when Mack had reluctantly departed. "Take off. Go pull up some weeds or something."

He shook his head. "Not on your life, Amanda. Where you go, I go. We're joined at the hip, partners in crime, whatever you prefer."

"That's ridiculous. I prefer to work alone. Besides, we can get more information more quickly if we're each working on different angles."

He grinned. "Nice try. A minute ago, you wanted me to go yank up weeds. Do you think that will help solve the case?"

"Okay, no. But you could go check land records or something, just in case Mrs. Cosgrove doesn't feel like telling me about her business deals."

Donelli hesitated. "I don't like it, Amanda. After what happened with the watch, it's entirely possible that the next attempt to stop you will be more direct. You could be in real danger."

"Does Mrs. Cosgrove seem like the type who'd stab me with a letter opener?"

"Maybe not, but I suggest you try not to forget the villains in *Arsenic and Old Lace*. They were sweet little old ladies, too."

"Okay, you've made your point. I won't drink or eat a thing while I'm there. Now, go."

"Meet me at your office no later than noon."

"I promise and if you get there first, don't you dare say anything to Oscar about what happened last night."

He sighed and backed away from the car. "Don't take any chances, Amanda."

"This is Mrs. Cosgrove I'm going to see. Not Jack the Ripper."

"I hope so," he said. He leaned in and kissed her with a passionate hunger that stunned her. The bruising, greedy kiss was a vivid reminder of how great a loss they'd risked lately. It also suggested he'd forgiven her for the previous night's stupid remarks. In letting her go weeks ago, in giving her the freedom to choose, he'd endangered everything extraordinary that had bonded them together over the last year. He'd been trusting her to realize it before it was too late.

Amanda was still shaking at the intensity of emotion his kiss had aroused when she finally shifted the car into gear and drove away. When she glanced back in the rearview mirror, she saw Donelli standing just where she'd left him, staring after her.

There was an eerie stillness about Mrs. Cosgrove's house. The windows were tightly shut, despite the warmth of the Indian summer day. No smoke curled from the chimney. Amanda rang the bell repeatedly, but there were no answering footsteps from within.

She walked slowly around the house, standing on tiptoe to peer into windows. There were no signs of life at all. A frisson of fear worked its chilling way down her spine as she rattled the knob on the kitchen door. It turned and the door swung open on creaky hinges. All things considered, she might have preferred that it remain tightly locked, she thought as she took a cautious step inside.

"Mrs. Cosgrove! It's Amanda Roberts. Are you home? May I come in?"

There was no response. She crept all the way in and went carefully through the kitchen. There were no dishes in the drain, but a peek into the refrigerator revealed cheese, eggs, milk, and a few other staples, indicating that she hadn't gone away.

At least not willingly.

The frightening thought popped into Amanda's head and wouldn't go away. She tiptoed down the hall into the parlor. There was no fire in the grate, and from the chill in the room it appeared that any blaze had died out long ago. Everything else seemed to be in place.

Then she remembered the cabinet. Wasn't that where any thief would wreak havoc? She made her way through the house to the display case, sighing with relief when she saw that it was locked and still filled with Mrs. Cosgrove's heirlooms. She was about to turn and leave when she heard the faint whisper of footsteps from the back of the house. Her pulse leapt and her palms turned slippery as she looked around for something to use as a weapon. There were all sorts of possibilities in the cabinet, but it was locked and she could just imagine what would happen if any more treasures vanished and her fingerprints were all over the damn doors. She grabbed the only available, likely object, a leaded crystal vase containing fresh chry-santhemums.

Positioning herself flat against the wall just inside the door, she waited as the incautious thump of footsteps grew steadily louder. Obviously, whoever it was saw no need to remain silent, possibly because he thought the house to be empty. Sunlight streaming through the entry hall cast a large, male shadow against the far wall. Amanda swallowed hard and tried to remind herself that shadows often exaggerate height. The reassurance didn't keep her heart from pounding wildly or her throat from going dry. Lifting the vase high, she waited for the man to step into the room.

When he did, she drove the heavy crystal in a downward arc, closing her eyes momentarily as it struck flesh with a resounding thunk that sent shock waves reverberating all the way up her arm.

"Dammit all, Amanda, are you out of your mind?"

"Mack?" Her voice turned the single word into a cry of relief and outrage. "What the hell are you doing here? I thought you went to the university."

"I started to, but I got nervous about you coming over here alone," he explained, wincing with pain as he rubbed his shoulder. Glass, flowers, and water lay in messy pools all over the floor.

"Why didn't you say something when I first got here?"

"I figured you'd be furious. I decided to wait outside, in case you needed me. I saw you go around the back of the house twenty minutes ago. When you didn't come back around, I got worried. Where's Mrs. Cosgrove?"

"I don't know. She's not downstairs. I haven't quite had the nerve to go upstairs looking for her."

"I'll go. You stay here and clean up the mess."

As much as she hated to admit it, she was glad he'd shown up. For all her bravado, she hadn't liked discovering the house all shut up the way it was and creeping around inside was every bit as hard on her nerves as getting shot at had been during the Chef Maurice murder investigation.

She was still standing right where Mack had left her, glass splintered all over the floor, when she heard him clomping noisily back down the stars.

"She's not up there either," he said. "Now let's get out of here before the cops show up and take us both in for breaking and entering."

"I didn't break, I only entered. The backdoor was unlocked."

He smiled every bit as ruefully as Donelli. "I doubt that's a distinction the police will take into account. Now let's go."

"Wait. As long as we're here, maybe I could just take a quick look at her business papers. If she's sold a lot of property lately, the contracts might still be around."

"Amanda," Mack began, but it was a weak protest, nowhere near as adamant as Donelli's would have been under the same circumstances. Much as she needed her ex-husband's cooperation in sifting through the papers all over Mrs. Cosgrove's desk, she regretted the discovery that his values were less rigid than Donelli's. It took him only about ten seconds to join her at the desk.

"What are we looking for?"

"Real estate papers. Deeds. Surveys. I don't know exactly."

"I assume that means I can skip over the grocery receipts."

She didn't even bother to respond to that. She just kept picking up stacks of paper, flipping through and setting them aside.

"Well, I'll be damned," Mack said.

"What?"

"Look at this. It's a contract on the old Milstead place."

"Let me see," Amanda said, grabbing for the papers. "This doesn't make any sense. That's the place Miss Martha's trying to save."

"Exactly."

"Maybe this is just the contract donating the land to Gwinnett County."

Mack had retrieved the legal binder from Amanda and was flipping through the pages. "Nope. There's no mention of the county in here, nor of the historical society."

"But she had promised that land to Miss Martha's preservation group. The request for designation as a historic landmark was filed ages ago and I know Miss Martha wouldn't have done that or launched the fund-raising campaign if there was any question about being able to get the property."

"I agree with you, Amanda, but from the looks of this Mrs. Cosgrove is about to double-cross her dear old friend."

CHAPTER
Fourteen

Still stunned by their discovery, Amanda reached for the papers, only to have Mack taunt her by holding them aloft and stepping beyond her reach.

"Mack!"

"Wait a second," he said. "Let me see if I can figure out who the buyer is."

"I am perfectly capable of reading a real estate document."

"So am I," he reminded her.

She knew all about possession and its status in law. She gave up arguing and tried peering over his shoulder. She couldn't see a thing. "What's it say?"

"It mentions a company, but the contract seems to be written to disguise any individuals involved."

"That makes perfect sense. Who'd want it known around these parts that they'd stolen a piece of property out from under Miss Martha's nose, especially after that huge fund-raising bash she threw the other night to save it. She wields a lot of political clout and she does not like being humiliated."

"Not even Miss Martha has enough clout to stop a perfectly legitimate sale from going through."

"No, but she does have enough to stop the buyer from getting the zoning permits needed to do anything with that land. I'd be willing to bet that the sale is contingent on getting some sort of zoning change."

Mack examined the fine print and grinned. "Here it is: Option shall be exercised and payment in full made on the date that all necessary zoning approvals are obtained from the county. Nice going, Amanda. The way your mind works truly is an amazing thing. With your straitlaced, middle-class background, how did you ever learn to think so deviously?"

"Hang around enough crooks and cheating husbands and you begin to catch on," she said, watching as the barb struck home. To her surprise she took little pleasure in the guilty flush that crept into Mack's cheeks.

"Amanda," he said, his voice dropping to the silky whisper that had once been capable of making her pulse race. Now, to her everlasting relief, it had no effect whatsoever.

She waved off what sounded like the beginning of yet another apology. "Not now, Mack. It's not the time."

He forced her chin up until her gaze was level with his. Blue eyes studied her intently. "Tell me the truth, Amanda. It's never going to be the right time for us, is it?"

She allowed herself an instant's regret before shaking her head. So many things were finally beginning to become clear to her. She'd held on to an illusion of what Mack had once been to her. She'd been young and giddily romantic when they'd met. She'd fallen for his easy charm and intellectual facade. The combination had seemed extraordinarily sexy. She was just beginning to realize that he didn't have the depth or the values of a man like Donelli. Donelli was solid, dependable. Their minds meshed, even when their techniques clashed. The clashes were as exciting in their own way as the finely tuned mental and physical joinings.

Relief washed over her at the realization that her pride, rather than her heart, had been hurt by Mack's defection two years ago. She was finally able to say in all honesty, "No, Mack. I think the time for us is past."

"Leaving you was the dumbest thing I ever did," he said ruefully.

"You'll get no argument from me on that," she said, then relented. She stood on tiptoe and kissed his cheek. "Stop beating yourself up over that, Mack. I have finally. I have a feeling that this is something we would have discovered sooner or later, anyway. You're happier with a nice orderly life that revolves around faculty teas and long hours spent in the University library. Your way of life doesn't include car bombs and death threats. Sooner or later you'd resent me for upsetting you all the time. My career would play havoc with yours.''

"And that's what you want? Car bombs and death threats?'' he inquired, his tone skeptical.

"Hardly that exactly, but I am willing to take the risks. I'm just not willing to include you or anyone else in the danger.''

"Not even the cop?''

"I can't answer that,'' she evaded. "Donelli makes his own decisions about things.''

"But you love him?''

She felt a grin begin to spread across her face. "Yeah,'' she admitted. "I guess I do. That doesn't mean it'll work out, though.''

Mack surprised her by apparently sensing her turmoil. He drew her into his arms. "If he has half the brains I think he has, it will be just fine. I hope you'll be happy, Amanda. I really do,'' he whispered. He kissed her lightly, a tentative exploration of possibilities. The touch of his lips didn't warm her as it once had. There was no desire left; the ashes of their once blazing passion had grown cold. Apparently convinced at last that there were no second chances for them, he drew away, his expression wistful.

Saddened by the loss, she rubbed her cheek against the

roughness of his sweater, taking in the scent of some classy aftershave that probably cost an arm and a leg and didn't do half as much to stir her blood as Donelli's natural, clean masculine scent. She sighed.

"Well, well, isn't this a touching scene?"

Amanda jerked away from Mack and turned to stare into the narrowed, angry eyes of Sheriff Eldon Mason.

"Sheriff . . ."

"Save it, Ms. Roberts."

"Now just a minute, Sheriff," Mack protested.

"You, too, Mr. Roberts. The two of you are already in enough trouble without blabbing away without a lawyer present."

"A lawyer?" Amanda repeated nervously. She could see how her presence in Mrs. Cosgrove's unattended home would look to a man to whom she'd promised to be on her best behavior, but surely he'd at least listen to her explanation without dragging out his Miranda card and reading her her rights.

"I'd say you could use one about now. Last night was a picnic compared to the plans I have for you today. How about we all go get into the cruiser and take a ride over to the station?"

"We could talk here," Amanda suggested hopefully. She had seen about as much of that one-cell jailhouse as she wanted to. She had the distinct impression that once Sheriff Mason got her over there this time, he just might not let her go.

"Nope. I like the idea of making this real official," he said, stepping toward them with a pair of handcuffs dangling from his fat fist. When he crunched several shards of the broken vase underfoot, he paused and looked down. "What happened here?"

Amanda used his momentary distraction as an opportunity to slip the real estate contract into her purse. It might not remain there long, if the sheriff had his way, but at least she'd have a shot at getting some evidence that could wrap up this whole conspiracy. All she needed was two minutes alone with a copying machine and a chance to sit down and have a long chat with Mrs. Cosgrove.

"Ms. Roberts, I asked you a question," the sheriff said, staring hard at her.

"Sorry. What?"

"What happened here? Any idea?"

"I just broke a vase."

Mack's brows rose at the innocent sound of that conveniently edited explanation. She had a feeling he was only barely resisting the urge to rub his shoulder.

"I'll clean it up," Amanda offered, hurriedly dropping to her knees.

"Leave it," the sheriff ordered sharply, wrapping a beefy hand around her upper arm and lifting her to her feet. "The crime lab boys will get it."

"Crime lab?" She thought that was slightly fancy terminology for the two deputies who alternated nights and weekends.

The sheriff apparently picked up on her sarcasm. "The *Atlanta* crime lab," he corrected, watching her closely for a reaction.

"Why would the Atlanta police be interested in a broken vase? It's not valuable. I'll pay for the stupid thing or pick up one just like it the next time I'm shopping. I'm sure Mrs. Cosgrove will understand."

"I doubt it, at least not for some time."

There was something very ominous in that. "Where is Mrs. Cosgrove?" she asked, trying not to let her nervousness show. She was very proud that her voice barely quivered.

"In the hospital. Somebody conked her over the head and left her for dead." He stared pointedly at the once solid and potentially lethal vase.

"What!" Mack and Amanda said in unison. "Where? Is she okay?"

He regarded them in disgust. "Your concern is touching. The doctors figure she will be just fine in a few days, no thanks to her attackers." Again, he shot a knowing look of condemnation at Amanda and Mack in turn.

"You're not suggesting that we did it with that vase, are you?" Amanda demanded, beginning to catch on to exactly how much trouble she and Mack might be in.

"The thought did cross my mind," the sheriff confessed cheerfully. "I wonder why? Even you have to admit that the theory does have a nice tidy ring of truth to it."

"But Mrs. Cosgrove wasn't even here when I got here."

"Because she was taken to the hospital about two hours ago," Sheriff Mason concurred. "A very short time after that a neighbor called up and reported that someone had broken into the house again. Lo and behold I drive back over and here you are."

"I did not whack that woman over the head," Amanda repeated, hoping that sooner or later the insistent denial would penetrate the sheriff's thick skull, which was covered once more with that disgusting cap of his. Admittedly, she had probably lost some credibility by what he might perceive as returning to the scene of her alleged original crime. She decided she'd better build up her alibi.

"Two hours ago I was at home. Mack can vouch for that and so can Joe Donelli. They were both there."

"I was there all night, in fact," Mack added. "Amanda never once left her bed."

That bit of information seemed to intrigue the sheriff. He snickered. "And here I thought you had the hots for Donelli."

Amanda wasn't sure which of the two men she ought to murder. Since Mack was at least attempting to provide her with an alibi, she excused his disclosure. As for the sheriff, she settled for informing him stiffly, "I'm not sure what speculation about my social life has to do with anything."

"It's a small town. It might be wise for you to remember

the implications of that. We don't miss much around here.''

''You missed whoever it was who knocked out Mrs. Cosgrove.''

His expression indignant, the sheriff whipped his hat off his head, rocked back on his heels, and said, ''Well, that's where you're wrong. I think I got me a couple of real good candidates right here.''

''Oh, for heaven's sake,'' Amanda snapped impatiently. ''Do you honestly think I would stick around after I tried to murder the woman?''

''You would if you didn't get what you came for.''

''What I came for?'' She clung a little more tightly to her purse.

''Sure. Like maybe those papers you tucked in your purse a minute ago, when you thought I wasn't paying attention.''

Amanda swore under her breath. She really had to stop selling these people short. Donelli was always on her case about that and obviously he was right. Sheriff Mason might sound and occasionally act like a stereotypical backwoods jerk, but he did have a college degree and ten years in law enforcement, all but the last few months, in fact, with the Atlanta PD. Donelli had taken great pleasure in informing her of that.

Right now, though, Eldon Mason was patiently holding out his hand. She doubted if he was simply hoping she'd shake it. Reluctantly, she turned over the papers. Sheriff Mason looked them over. Without even asking what they meant, he folded them and stuck them into his back pocket. Either he understood the connection to the case or he just wanted to keep them out of Amanda's reach.

"Shall we go, folks."

It didn't really sound like a question. He was already heading for the door and Amanda seriously doubted if he planned to walk out without them. She lingered a minute, just in case.

"Now, Ms. Roberts."

"Coming, Sheriff," she muttered, casting one last, longing look back at the desk. She had a feeling that still buried in that messy pile of papers was the one last piece she needed for the puzzle—a scribbled note, a check stub, something that would tell her exactly who was buying that land from Mrs. Cosgrove.

And that bit of information would lead her straight to the person behind all the thefts.

CHAPTER
Fifteen

"Not again, Amanda." Donelli's expression was long-suffering as he walked into the tiny police station and found her exhaustedly sipping at her fifth cup of Sheriff Mason's pathetic excuse for coffee. It was almost as bad as Miss Martha's weak tea. She'd finished her last jelly bean an hour before and acid was churning in her stomach. She was thrilled to see him, but she was in no mood for his sarcasm.

"Don't start on me, Donelli," she warned. "What are you doing here anyway?"

"Oscar caught up with me at the courthouse. He said you were in trouble—again. Since he couldn't leave the office because of a production meeting, he suggested I drop by and bail you out—again."

"What a peach," she grumbled, too tired to even be alarmed that Oscar knew where she was and most likely why. She was going to have this whole thing wrapped up in a day or two anyway, so even if he suspended her, it wouldn't be for long. She hoped.

"How'd he find out?"

"Eldon called. I think he was hoping that someone with more influence with you than I apparently have would get you to behave."

"Is Oscar furious?"

"What do you think? Apparently you've blown the hell out of your deadline. The publisher is on his case. The production manager is livid. The circulation manager is having heart palpitations. And you're in jail. Even you have to admit this is wearing a little thin. He thought he hired a reporter, not some crazy woman who's addicted to hanging out in police stations."

"Are those your words or his?" Judging from Donelli's expression, that was probably not the best thing she could have asked. "Never mind. Just get us out of here."

"Us?"

She gestured toward Mack, who was slouched down in one of the straight-backed metal chairs, flipping through a five-year-old magazine. It was a *Sports Illustrated* swimsuit issue. Its presence in this backwater jail with its macho manpower didn't surprise her. Mack's fascination with it did. Until his fling with the sophomore, Mack had been far more interested in curving fluctuations in the Dow Jones average than he had been in extended studies of any female anatomy other than hers.

Donelli perched on the edge of the desk closest to Amanda and said, ''I think you'd better explain how the two of you wound up here this time.''

''The sheriff seems to think that Mack and I tried to kill Mrs. Cosgrove.''

Even Donelli, whose faith in her was generally unshakable, seemed taken aback by that blunt announcement. To his way of thinking, cops did not generally make such charges without cause. ''Why the devil would he think a thing like that? What the hell have you two been doing since I left you earlier?''

''We haven't been doing anything. *Somebody* bopped Mrs. Cosgrove on the head and the sheriff found Mack and me standing within inches of the remains of what might have made a very good weapon. Not that it was the weapon, of course. The vase actually got broken because I tried to hit Mack over the head with it, before I realized it was Mack, of course. Remember, he said he was going to the University? Only he didn't, so when he came sneaking in, I clobbered him. I missed his head and hit him in the shoulder. I didn't hit Mrs. Cosgrove at all.'' She paused for breath. ''Am I making any sense?''

''Actually, you are, which scares the daylights out of me because it means I'm starting to think the way you do.''

''I knew our compatibility would come in handy someday. Now can you get us out of here?''

"Have you been booked?"

"No."

"Did anyone read you your rights?"

"No. I think he meant to, but he got distracted by all the glass."

Donelli groaned. "Where's Sheriff Mason?"

"Beats me. He got a call and went tearing out of here. He told us to stay where we were."

"Without putting you into a cell or leaving a deputy in charge?"

"You mean there's no one outside either?"

"Not that I noticed."

Amanda shrugged. "Apparently he trusts us."

"Or he knows perfectly well that he has no cause to hold you and he's counting on you to stick around until he finds the evidence he needs. My suggestion is that we all get the hell out of here before he comes back."

"Are you sure he won't shoot us for attempted escape?"

"He might, but I'd say it's a slimmer risk than most of the ones you take."

"Then let's go."

"Do either of you have a car here?"

"Nope. They're both back at Mrs. Cosgrove's."

No one seemed especially pleased about that, least of all Mack.

It was an uncomfortable ride. Donelli kept casting condemning looks at Mack as if he were the one responsible for getting the two of them dragged into jail. Mack was

drumming his fingers against the armrest and keeping his
attention focused on some spot that did not include Donelli
in his peripheral vision. He might be giving Amanda up
without a fight, but he obviously wasn't pleased about
watching it happen under his nose. She almost felt sorry
for him. She knew how much it hurt to watch someone
you loved ride off into the sunset with someone else. It
had taken her two long years to get over Mack doing the
exact same thing to her. There might be a certain sense
of justice in this current turnabout, but she didn't feel much
like gloating. Instead, she asked Donelli, "Did you find
anything at the courthouse?"

"I found out that a corporation called First Starts has
applied to have a chunk of Mrs. Cosgrove's land zoned
for a strip mall."

"The Milstead property," Amanda guessed.

Donelli stared at her. "Good God, you're right. I was
so busy studying the zoning application, I didn't think
about what might be on the property now. Why would she
stab Miss Martha in the back like that?"

"She must be more desperate for money than I realized.
What's the status of the application?"

"It's already been approved by the zoning board. The
final public hearing is in two weeks."

"Who's behind the corporation?"

"I have somebody in Atlanta checking that out. I should
know later this afternoon. Did you find anything at Mrs.
Cosgrove's?"

"A contract on the land. It mentioned the same company, I think. That was it, wasn't it, Mack?" She glanced over her shoulder. He was staring out the window. "Mack, was that the name of the company? First Starts?"

He nodded. "Yes."

"Anyway," she told Donelli, "the contract indicated that the sale was contingent on the zoning approval."

"Maybe we ought to take a ride into Atlanta and stop by the newspapers to see if the library has anything on this First Starts outfit," Donelli suggested.

"My thoughts exactly."

"Do you need me to help with that?" Mack asked, apparently tired of listening to the two of them share the same wavelength.

"No. We can handle it," Amanda said.

"Then drop me off at the car and I'll talk to you later. Maybe I'll go by the hospital to see how Mrs. Cosgrove's doing."

"Good idea. Call me at the office to let me know. We should be back there within a couple of hours or you can leave a message with Jenny Lee."

Mack nodded curtly to Donelli as he got out, then reached through the window to touch Amanda lightly on the cheek. "Take care, sweetheart. I hope you find everything you're looking for."

"You, too, Mack. Thanks for standing by me last night and this morning."

"Anytime. Talk to you later."

To Donelli's credit he didn't ask why the conversation had sounded so final. In fact, he didn't say anything as they drove to the newspaper office. He even left it to Amanda to get them into the library. She flashed her magazine credentials at the security guard. That got them as far as a clerk in the library, who wanted to know how they'd gotten upstairs.

"The security guard cleared us."

"Sorry," she said. "That was a mistake. We don't let outsiders use the library."

"It's an emergency," Amanda said. "Please, as a professional courtesy to *Inside Atlanta*, couldn't you make an exception just this once?"

"I'll ask," she finally said grudgingly. "Wait here."

"She is not a happy woman," Donelli observed as she went in search of the librarian.

"Maybe her mood would have improved if you'd flashed one of your charming smiles at her."

"I tried," he admitted. "You just didn't see me. It didn't work. I must be losing my touch."

Amanda's delicate blond eyebrows rose a fraction of an inch, but she managed to keep her sarcastic retort to herself.

It took several more minutes before the girl finally returned. "Sorry. No exceptions. The main library has the back copies on microfilm. You can see that."

"Damn," Amanda muttered, seeing absolutely no point in lingering to battle with the clerk. "Let's go."

By the time they reached the downtown library, her patience was wearing thin. The index to the Atlanta papers contained two references to First Starts. With Donelli standing over her, she put the first one into the machine and wound the microfilm to the right page.

They found a mention of the company in an article on a recent meeting of the zoning board. It indicated that the company's request for a change in zoning had been approved unanimously and sent on for full county approval. There was no news there. Donelli had gotten that much in his search at the courthouse.

It was the second item—a small box on the business pages only three months earlier—that really caught Amanda's attention.

"Joe," she whispered. "Look at this."

First Starts, it seemed, had been formed as a minority-owned business and had applied for applicable loans from the federal government. None of the names mentioned as officers of the new company were familiar, but the name of the man who'd been advising them was:

"First Starts managements credits one man with guiding them during their formation: Henry Taylor Jr."

"Well, I'll be damned," Donelli muttered.

"It fits," Amanda said, her excitement mounting. "Jessica Taylor taking the flag, all of it is finally coming together."

"Let's go have another talk with Mr. Taylor."

* * *

Mr. Taylor did not care to talk to a reporter and a private investigator. Through his secretary, he referred them to his lawyer. Donelli was not used to being dismissed. He did not take kindly to it.

"Excuse us, sweetheart," he said to the secretary who was bravely blocking the way to Mr. Taylor's door.

"You can't go in there," she said stubbornly. "He doesn't want to see you."

"Too bad," Joe said without a qualm. He lifted the girl, moved her out of the way, and set her back down. With a cry of outrage, she reached for the security buzzer under her desk.

"There's no need for that," Donelli advised. "We won't take long."

He walked into Henry Taylor's office, Amanda right behind him. Henry Taylor was pacing the room. His cool, confident demeanor of their last meeting was a thing of the past. He had the terrified look of a hunted animal.

"You have no right to come barging in here," he said, reaching for his own security buzzer.

"Don't bother. Your secretary's already called for them," Donelli said. "Why don't you sit down and tell us about First Starts, while we wait?"

Taylor's struggle against some inner demon showed in his eyes. Finally giving up, he sank down in the expensive leather chair behind his desk and put his face in his hands.

When he looked up again, his expression was resigned, almost relieved, in fact. It was as if he'd known this day was coming and was glad to see it over with.

"What do you want to know?" he asked as the door burst open and two security guards came through, guns drawn.

"Do you want them to hear this?" Donelli inquired, gesturing toward the guards.

Again, the banker appeared uncertain. He could have seized the out and bought himself a little more time. Apparently he decided it wasn't worth the effort. He held up a hand. "Gentlemen, it's all right. My secretary made a mistake. Everything is fine here."

The larger of the two appeared disappointed. "Are you sure, Mr. Taylor? We can get them out of here." He cracked his knuckles.

"It's not necessary. They're just here to discuss some business."

"Okay. We'll wait right outside, though. You call if you need us." He gave Donelli a menacing look. Donelli smiled back.

"Thanks, you can go now," Mr. Taylor said hurriedly.

As soon as they'd left and closed the door behind them, Amanda extracted a notebook from her purse. "This is on the record, Mr. Taylor."

He nodded. "I assumed as much."

"First, what is your role in First Starts?" she asked.

"I've helped them organize, advised them on loan applications, that sort of thing."

It all sounded fairly routine and innocent, hardly the kind of thing to have Henry Taylor looking panicky. "And?" she persisted.

"I don't understand."

"Mr. Taylor, do you have a financial stake in the company?"

"I am not on the Board of Directors, if that's what you're asking."

"I'm sure you're not," she agreed. "That might impede the company's ability to apply for loans as a minority-controlled firm, isn't that right?"

"Yes, but . . ."

"Are you a silent investor, Mr. Taylor?"

He drew in a deep breath. "Yes, I have a small amount invested in the company."

"How small?"

"A few thousand dollars. It's insignificant."

"So insignificant that you were willing to impugn the sanity of several women, one of them your stepmother, and set me up as a thief in order to assure that the historical society wouldn't put up a credible fight over the Milstead property?"

There was a flare of indignation in his eyes. "You're not going to lay that one on me, Ms. Roberts. I would never do such a thing, especially to my own stepmother.

My concern about her mental competence was brought on by a number of incidents, very real incidents. I love her. I have simply tried to protect her, as best I could.''

"From whom?''

"Herself.''

Amanda shook her head. "I don't think so, Mr. Taylor. Your stepmother is every bit as sane as you or I. Who are you protecting?''

Donelli had been observing the banker closely during this exchange. "I think I know the answer to that, Amanda. It's your wife, isn't it?'' he prodded gently. "She was after the money.''

To Amanda's horror, Henry Taylor seemed to crumple before their eyes. Bitter tears welled up. "I know how it must seem to you, but she is not a bad woman. I think she just married me expecting so much more than I've been able to give her.''

"You have an incredible home, a fine standing in the community, two bright daughters. What more could she want?'' Amanda said.

"It's never been enough. We're always in debt and she's always resented my stepmother for putting us in that position.''

"So, she saw First Starts as a way to get even and get ahead at the same time?''

He shook his head. "No, not at all. She doesn't even know about my involvement with the company.''

Amanda stared at him. "She doesn't know? Then I don't understand."

"Frankly, neither do I," Donelli said. "Was she or wasn't she involved in this whole scheme to keep the Milstead place from being declared a historic landmark?"

"No, that had nothing to do with her. She was only interested in having my stepmother seem incompetent, so I could go into court and ask to be made guardian of the estate."

"Did she steal the flag?"

"Yes."

"Who put it back?"

"I did. I was able to find one. I tried to make it look old. I hated to see Mother so upset. I didn't think she'd be able to tell the difference."

"Your wife didn't know about the substitute?"

"No."

"Did you know she tried to sell the original?"

"I guessed as much. I assume she saw it as a way not only to get the money, but to make Mother seem dotty as well."

"And none of that has anything to do with First Starts?"

"Nothing, I assure you."

"So who is behind it, Mr. Taylor?" Donelli asked impatiently. "Let's cut to the bottom line on all of this. Who's really bankrolling that company?"

He blanched at the attack. "I can't tell you," he said

in a voice so weak Amanda could barely hear him. "I can't. I'd be ruined."

"You will be anyway. If you don't tell us, you're going to take the fall."

"So be it," he said with an air of defeat.

Suddenly, pieces of the puzzle began falling into place for Amanda. Only one person had the power to manipulate all of this. And only one person stood to lose everything if his involvement were disclosed.

"Come on, Donelli. I have an idea."

"Amanda!"

"Come on! He's told us everything he's going to tell us."

Donelli left the bank with her, but the instant they were outside he yanked her to a halt and snapped, "Would you mind telling me what this is all about? He was ready to talk."

"He wouldn't have talked if you'd held lit matches to his fingertips. Couldn't you see that the man was terrified?"

"With Henry Taylor, it seems to be a perpetual state of mind. Underneath all that polish, he's a weak, sniveling coward. How could he let his wife do those things to his stepmother?"

"Henry Taylor's lousy personality and values are not the issue. We've got bigger fish to fry."

"What are you thinking, Amanda?"

"Who has enough clout around here to influence the

county, the banking community, even the federal officials?''

She watched as the implications of her question sank in. An incredulous look spread across Donelli's face. ''Donald Wellington?''

''Looks that way to me. Care to confront the senator in his den?''

''I think we'd better have a little more to go on before we go charging into his office with an accusation like this. Can you imagine the repercussions if we're wrong?''

''We're not wrong. And I wasn't thinking of his office. I thought perhaps we should all have tea at Miss Martha's.'' She grinned. ''Sounds intriguing, doesn't it?''

''Amanda, I admire your spunk, but are you sure Miss Martha's up to this?''

''I think when she finds out what her precious nephew has been up to, there won't be a legal authority in the land who can protect him from her wrath.''

Donelli's smile widened at the prospect of nailing a corrupt elected federal official to the wall. ''Let's do it.''

CHAPTER

Sixteen

Miss Martha was nearly apoplectic with rage.

"I will kill that boy," she said, thumping the floor resoundingly with her cane. Her blue eyes snapped with anger. "How dare Donald interfere with my plans for that property."

"We don't actually have any proof that he's behind it," Amanda cautioned.

"But you know he is, the same as I do, or you wouldn't be here. I can recognize a snake when it crawls right past my feet. That boy has been slinking around here for months now, trying to talk me out of this preservation fight. I couldn't imagine why he'd want to do that. He kept telling me all the excitement was bad for my health, which is absolute hogwash. I've never been healthier in my life and there's nothing I like better than a good challenge.''

"Miss Martha, are you sure you're up to a confrontation, though?'' Donelli asked, his expression concerned. Obviously he'd noted the high color in her cheeks and her increasing agitation. It was worrying Amanda, as well.

"He is your nephew,'' Amanda said. "This is bound to put a terrible strain on you.''

"Don't you worry about me, young lady. All I have to do is think about Henrietta lying in that hospital bed with a lump on her head and I'll be ready to take him apart with my bare hands.''

"Maybe you'd better leave justice to the sheriff's office and the courts,'' Amanda said.

"This is a family matter,'' Miss Martha insisted.

"Not when it involves a U.S. senator, stolen property, conspiracy, fraud, and who knows what else.''

"We'll worry about all those legalities, after I finish with putting that young man in his place. Now let's just gather everyone over here and put an end to this nonsense right now. I'll have Della make the calls.''

"What if Henry Taylor warns the senator?'' Donelli said. "Maybe it would be better not to invite him to this meeting.''

"He must be here,'' Miss Martha contradicted. "Don't worry about it. Donald won't pay a bit of attention to Henry, even if he does tell him he suspects something's up. Donald always thought he was an old fool. If they've been in cahoots on this, it's only because Donald finally found a way to use him. Besides, Donald is far too cocky to consider the possibility that we might really be on to him.''

Sure enough, Della reported that Donald Wellington was on his way, as was his administrative assistant, along with Ellie Mae Taylor, her stepson, Henry's wife, and William Davenport.

Donelli seemed puzzled by the last name on the list. ''Why Davenport, Amanda?''

She avoided looking directly at Miss Martha. She was sure the color in her cheeks now had nothing to do with her agitation at Donald. ''Because he can identify the woman who brought in the Jefferson Davis gun. My guess is that it was somebody on Donald's staff, most likely his assistant. One of these days, I'm probably going to have to go over to Ellie Mae's and apologize to Deborah for suspecting her.'' She shuddered at the prospect.

''What about Mack?'' Miss Martha said, glancing cautiously at Donelli. ''Don't you think he deserves to be in on the finale?''

Amanda doubted that Mack wanted to be in the same room with Donelli and her again for any reason, but she nodded. ''I'll give him a call.''

To her surprise, he accepted. He must have been even fonder of Miss Martha's insipid tea than she'd realized.

So, she thought as she hung up, the game had been set in motion. All that was left was the waiting. It was not her favorite thing to do. To keep occupied, she called Oscar. He was not overjoyed to hear from her.

"I didn't think they allowed you more than one call from jail," he muttered. She could hear him hunting and pecking at the keys of his computer. Either he was trying frantically to write something for the next edition or he couldn't wait to finish the memo suspending her.

"I'm not in jail," she informed him.

He sighed heavily with obvious regret. "So, Donelli bailed you out again. You'd better not let that guy get away, Amanda. He's the only man I know who's likely to put up with you."

"I'll keep your advice in mind, Oscar. Now are you the least bit interested in the reason I called?"

"Not unless it has to do with filling the middle section of *Inside Atlanta*."

"It does. I think you're going to like the headline, too. Oh, and you might want to dust off a file photo of Senator Wellington."

The soft click of the computer keys fell silent. Apparently she finally had his full attention. "Go on."

"It appears that Donald is behind everything that's been happening. I can't get into all of it now. He's already on his way to Miss Martha's for a showdown."

"Well, I'll be damned," he breathed softly. "I never did like that pretentious jerk. Couldn't imagine how he and Miss Martha came from the same family. You hold down the fort, Amanda. I'll be there in twenty minutes."

"Oscar, you can't get out of the parking lot that fast."

"I'll be there. Don't you dare start without me. Call Larry. If he's not home, he might be out at the *Gazette*. I gave him an assignment to do out there this week. I want pictures of this. Hell, tell him to bring color."

Obviously she'd stirred the printer's ink in his blood. Oscar's administrative style might infuriate her, but at heart he was a solid newsman with the guts to go for the jugular when it was called for. The impending downfall of a U.S. senator appeared to be one of those times.

"I'll do my best to track Larry down, but don't count on him, Oscar. Bring a camera from the office. You know how to shoot pictures when you have to."

"Right. I'll be there soon."

Back in the parlor, Amanda found Della setting out a silver tea service and Miss Martha's best china cups. A tray of petits fours had materialized, along with one of Della's sour cream pound cakes and a whole plate of miniature pecan pies. Pristine damask napkins were neatly arranged alongside the sterling silver spoons. An arrangement of fresh flowers had been brought over from the dining room. If the party had been in the planning for weeks, it couldn't have been any more elegant.

"I think that should do it, Della," Miss Martha said, nodding in satisfaction.

"I'll be bringing you refills for the teapot every so often," Della said. "You just call if you need anything in the meantime."

Della had no sooner left the room when the doorbell rang. Amanda jumped nervously. Miss Martha gave her a faint smile. "Well, my dear, the web is spun. Shall we see who'll be caught in it?"

Mr. Davenport arrived first, followed quickly by the Taylors. They turned up separately but managed to hide their surprise at finding the others there. Henry took one look at Donelli and Amanda and turned pale. After glancing toward Miss Martha for permission, he went to her brandy decanter and poured himself a drink. The silence in the room grew thicker with each passing second.

"Why are we here?" Jessica Taylor asked, casting a nervous glance at William Davenport.

"To have tea, of course," Miss Martha said with such an innocent air that Amanda almost believed her. "Do try some of Della's pound cake. It's her specialty."

Jessica took a wafer-thin slice and proceeded to mash it to bits unconsciously as she continued to stare toward the front door. Each time the bell rang, she winced. Ironically, when Oscar and Larry turned up, she appeared to calm down.

"Miss Martha, is this another one of your fund-raising efforts?" she said. "You should have said something. I didn't bring along my checkbook. Did you, Henry?"

Henry kept his eyes trained on Donelli and shook his head.

"Henry, dear, you don't look well," Miss Martha observed. "Do sit down. Have you been working too hard?"

He sat down reluctantly next to his stepmother. Ellie Mae patted his hand. "He always has been a hard worker," she said.

Oscar kept circling the room like an anxious father waiting for his daughter to get home from her first date.

"Amanda, could I speak to you for a minute?" he said finally. "Excuse us, folks. We have to take care of a little business."

He half dragged her from the room. "Is the senator coming or not?"

"He'll be here."

"And you've got hard evidence that he's done whatever the hell it is you think he's done."

Amanda forced herself to look Oscar straight in the eye when she admitted, "Not exactly."

"What!" he exploded just as the front door burst open. Donald Wellington, sporting the casually elegant look that had courted female votes on the campaign trail, came hurrying in. He was followed by his administrative assistant, Mildred Layton, an older, heavyset woman, who had a reputation for political savvy and organizational skills. Amanda realized that she could easily have been the woman who took the gun to Willoughby's. Mack arrived only a few paces behind them.

"Aunt Martha, are you all right?" Donald asked solicitously.

"Don't look so worried, Donald. I'm fine. Would you

care for some tea? Mildred, what about you? Tea with lemon, I recall.''

Donald looked irritated by his aunt's offhand demeanor. Mildred seemed confused. ''Miss Wellington, Donald really doesn't have the time . . .''

Miss Martha's hard stare stopped her in mid-sentence. ''What I mean to say is that he had to cancel an important engagement to rush over here. It was our understanding that this was urgent.''

''I assure you it is. A very grave matter has come to my attention and I wanted to bring together a few of my most ardent supporters to plan our strategy. It appears that someone has convinced Henrietta to sell the old Milstead place for a shopping mall.''

Ellie Mae gasped in dismay. ''Why on earth would she do something like that?''

''That's something only she can answer. In the meantime, it is my understanding that there is still time to prevent this travesty from taking place. I intend to appear before the county to protest this zoning change. I assume all of you will be there with me.''

''Absolutely,'' Ellie Mae said. Mr. Davenport nodded at once.

Henry Taylor looked as though he wanted to dig a hole and crawl into it. He got up and poured himself another brandy. Jessica's teacup rattled against its saucer.

Miss Martha turned a guileless gaze on her nephew. ''Donald? I can count on you, can't I?''

"Aunt Martha, why can't you just let it be? You've saved half a dozen buildings that were destined for demolition. What possible difference can that old falling down cabin make?"

"That old falling down cabin is our history, Donald, and you'd best not be forgetting it."

"It is standing in the way of progress."

"I assume you're referring to First Starts," she said.

"First Starts?" he repeated blankly. Amanda had to admire his gall. He carried off the innocent act with aplomb.

"The company attempting to rezone the property," Miss Martha informed him.

"Never heard of it. Is there some reason I should have?"

The senator's act was even better than Amanda had anticipated. In fact, it was beginning to make her very nervous. What if she'd been wrong about all this? What if it hadn't been Donald Wellington behind the scam at all?

Suddenly Jessica Taylor started to laugh. It was not a particularly pleasant sound. The sound built and built toward hysteria. Her husband stared at her helplessly. It was Mack who finally walked over and gave her a sharp, sobering slap.

"That's enough, Jess."

"But don't you see, Mack? They thought it was the noble senator. They thought Donald was behind First Starts, when it was you and I all along."

Amanda felt the room begin to spin. She looked into Mack's eyes, pleading for it to be a lie, but the truth was written all over his face. "Mack? How could you?" she whispered, finally ending the astonished hush in the room.

There was no hint of apology in his shrug. "Jessica likes expensive things," he said. "Isn't that right?"

"Oh, God," Amanda moaned, burying her face in her hands. Mack and Jessica Taylor? She had to be at least ten years older. She was married. And from what Henry Taylor had admitted earlier she was not above using sleazy tactics to get whatever she wanted. What she wanted apparently was money, the more the better. Mack, no doubt, had been a means to an end. Or was it the other way around?

As she sat there trying to sort through the horror of the discovery, she sensed that Donelli was quietly clearing the room. She was aware of footsteps and whispers, but she couldn't bear to face anyone, least of all her ex-husband.

"Amanda," Mack said.

She looked up at him then, feeling emptier than she had at any time in the weeks after the divorce. "I never knew you at all, did I?"

"No," he said and this time there was a hint of sorrow in his voice. "Maybe if you had, there would have been a way to save me from myself. I wanted too much, Amanda, and I knew how to go about getting it. All I needed was someone who understood that, someone who'd work with me. You couldn't do that. You were always too honest. When I saw the way you went after those corrupt judges in Manhattan, I knew things would always have to be by the book around you. I did you a favor by leaving you."

She nodded. "Yes. I'm not sure you meant to, but I think you did." She wanted to leave, wanted to get as far away from him as possible, but there were answers she had to hear first.

"Did Jessica steal the gun?"

"No, I did that. She took it to Willoughby's."

"But William Davenport didn't recognize her."

"She wore a disguise that time."

"And the watch?"

"I planted it and called the sheriff. I needed to get you off that story. I should have known it wouldn't work."

"Why did you tell me where the gun was? You might have gotten away with five or six million dollars, if it had actually been auctioned off."

"We were going to get plenty out of this land deal. I meant what I told you at the time; it was a gesture, a peace offering."

The twisted logic of that almost made her physically sick. Then she thought of Mrs. Cosgrove and felt like screaming. "Mack, did you knock out Henrietta Cosgrove?"

For the first time there was the faintest suggestion of guilt in his eyes. "Yes, I had to get to those papers before you did, but I didn't have time to find them. Then once you'd seen them, I knew the whole thing was bound to unravel. I'm almost glad it's over. I'm just sorry I had to betray you all over again. If you never believe another word I say, believe that."

"You didn't betray me, Mack. You betrayed yourself. You have a brilliant mind. You should have put it to better use."

"Not all of us are cut out for noble causes, Amanda. Stick with your cop. You two are meant for each other."

She glanced toward the doorway and saw Donelli waiting. "Yes," she said softly. "I think we are."

"Are you going to marry him?"

"He hasn't asked."

"He will."

She smiled. "You know me, Mack. I'll worry about that when the time comes."

"Don't back away because of what happened between us. I'm a lousy basis for comparison."

"What I felt for you is all in the past," she said truthfully. "The man I loved didn't even exist."

He stood up then. "I guess this is good-bye." He started to bend down to kiss her, then shook his head and backed off a step. "Stay out of trouble, Amanda."

She thought she heard a catch in his voice, but that couldn't be because Mack never had been one to show his emotions. She watched him walk away with a lump in her throat, but no more regrets. It was truly over, once and for all. She turned toward where Donelli was still standing, waiting, leaning against the doorway.

Patient, easygoing Donelli. Nothing in his nonchalant posture indicated that he'd had the slightest doubt about her ability to handle this final good-bye between her and Mack. Only when she looked down did she realize that his hands were clenched into fists. Only when he got closer did she detect the tiny white lines of tension around his drawn mouth. He tried to smile, but it faltered.

"You okay?" he asked.

"I feel as if I've gone ten rounds with that tractor of yours and lost. Did you know?"

"About Mack? No. I was just as convinced as you were that it was the senator. I should have realized that Mack's background in economics would have made him privy to all sorts of information about minority businesses and federal loans. That, combined with his access to Miss Martha and the others, should have made him a prime suspect. Maybe I just wanted to trust him for your sake."

"Or maybe your instincts are getting bogged down in fertilizer."

He grinned. "Maybe so. Maybe I'll give some more thought to bringing them out of retirement, after all. I'm sure Meredith Walters will hire me again."

"Speaking of Meredith, exactly how well do you know her?"

"Jealous?"

"No. Just curious."

"Sure."

"How well, Donelli?"

"Actually, I've never met her. I was hired by her boss. I was assigned to a case once before involving the auction house. He knew I'd moved down here."

She stared at him indignantly. "You let me go all these weeks thinking you once had the hots for Meredith."

"Just a small lesson in the dangers of jumping to conclusions."

"Don't hold your breath. Old habits die hard."

"So I've noticed."

"It was over with Mack even before this afternoon, Donelli. I hope you believe that."

His grin was cockier now. "I knew that all along. You didn't."

"So," she began, rubbing her fingers over his knuckles until his hand curved tightly around hers. "Where do we go from here, Donelli?"

"A church," he suggested with a hopeful gleam in his eyes.

"That might be a little drastic."

He shook his head. "No compromises this time, Amanda. It's all or nothing."

She thought of what Mack had said, even Oscar's paternal advice. Most of all she remembered the long lonely nights without Donelli by her side. She took a deep breath. What the hell. She always had been a risk-taker. Besides, the decision had been made months ago really. It had just taken her until now to realize it. She linked her arm through his and smiled. "Let's go then." She shot a challenging gaze up. "But if you try serving corn on the cob at our reception, it'll be the shortest marriage on record."

"Sweet potato pie?"

"Cake, Donelli. One of those many-tiered cakes with a little bride and groom on the top. That's it. No compromises."

"Chocolate cake?"

"Okay, one compromise."

He patted her cheek. "This should work out just fine, Amanda."

"Should we go tell Oscar and Larry?"

"If they're the kind of journalists I think they are, they're probably already waiting at the church."